THE
DEAD SEA
SOULS

THE
DEAD SEA
SOULS

DOUGLAS K.
PEARSON

Dead Sea Souls
© 2010 Douglas K. Pearson
Storymakers, LLC

Edited by David Egner
Cover design by AUXILIARY Advertising & Design
Book design and layout: Dave Gilman

Printed in the United States of America
10 11 12 13 /CS/ 10 9 8 7 6 5 4 3 2 1

He was given power to make war against the
saints and to conquer them.

This is the accurate record of the Last Helmsman. My log verifies the accounts of the five disturbed souls who escaped the genocide, and braved releasing their mutter-ings for the ship's log.

As Head of the Last Watch, I not only sail across blackest night, but enter the abysmal darkness of the minds of the res-cued.

I shelter my family from these stories. They need protection. They are weak from seeing the crushing weight of great peril.

About the end? We aren't blown up in a bang, nor do we fade away in fizzle.

It but comes as the Inspired-Horrible, havoc their reek of dismay and disgust upon the screaming.

I now give this accurate story and logbook of endurance to show that Evil turns on itself in that final dark hour before the return of God.

I give it to you because what we know in our hearts will save us. Just because it is our future doesn't mean we have to share in the terror.

1

The Dead Sea Souls

I unhook my cold, hard hands from the helm and work the stiffness out of them for we are seafaring in the deep of night, atop icy waters. All is dark black, but my eyes are adjusted and my heart is seasoned. I can see shapes in the water and feel the haunt of great suffering. Both raise my skin in chill.

We are ghost-sailors. My family hugs the ice-lines of desolate places as if mere ice can remind us of how it once was. How people once had lived. How we once had inhabited and worked the land. How we once had shared and even loved. We hold the icelines because more than ever, my parents need reminders that their memories are true.

I turn our ocean-going sailboat a few degrees to port for no given reason, and our hull glides by the torso of a woman. Our wake swirls and spins her body in a circle and for a moment, she faces me.

Through the darkness, I see the soft glow of ice crystals stuck to her nose and eyelashes as if broken glass had been glued to her face. Her hair is gray with frost. Her eyes are but dark dead purple circles and they are as despairing as the black water that covers what is left of her body. The blood red moon beyond the dirt clouds skews the details of her face. We sail by and she is gone.

It has come to pass.

I turn away from other frost-covered countenances of frozen dead who float and catch the weak albedo, which can only illumine the subtle sparkle of skin. All faces appear like spent light bulbs.

All horror films ever made are coming true.

They are shown to me in short clips, as stretched and faded as the storytellers themselves. They are unspooled to me as I command the Fourth Watch and work to sail through the endlessness of the black, predawn darkness.

I write every finding into the ship's log because we have nowhere else to dump the misery of the four we have rescued.

Some of them stare wide-eyed across the ocean as we sail through the darkest times of this night. Others are comatose and all are in deep need of a slumber that will not come.

My hand shakes as I write. My fingers shiver in cold and fear. I hate the fear more than the sting of frost. For when I am afraid, I look at the floating dead. I see their twisted mouths and holes in their faces where birds have taken their eyes. Only then do I turn away, because if I don't, my heart will despair and I will become as dead as the bloated corpses.

If I don't turn away, I will lose hope and be like those aboard who cannot talk and can only stare into the wind.

My mother tells my brothers and sister that a great storm has come and washed the dead to the sea. She has said it so many times that she believes it herself.

I hear her repeating, "Shhh. The storm will soon pass." I hear her soothing whisper every time I go below. I go down to smile at my little brothers and sister. I do not interrupt my mother because it is easier for her to believe her own story; her belief that only storms kill the dead. She ignores the many frozen arms that hold Bibles up out of the water.

If we are granted more time, she may teach the young ones different. She may speak the truth like my father used to say to me. A lot of good it did him.

But it did me good. I do know the truth. I see it in how the dead are grouped together. The truth is clear.

The dead were dumped.

They were dumped when they were still alive.

It wasn't a bad storm or a killer wave. It was the human heart that did this. The human heart at its very worst.

I want to find out how these happenings came to be. I hope to make record of it in our logbook.

Our heavy sailboat has now become a life raft. We no longer forge lines through dead bodies like we do an ice flow.

We have found survivors!

Stragglers of the bygone who have found a way to cheat the thermal cold are aboard. They are damaged goods who always want more than our scant rations allow, but beating hearts nonetheless!

I am the first mate and The Last Helmsman of the Fourth Watch. I navigate our sailboat, Defiance, through the Dead Sea Souls.

League of the Intolerant

A s the frozen corpses thump along our hull, they whisper fate. They rumor that God is releasing an apocalypse and for some reason, some of us are still alive. Whisper and rumor.

For every hundred years or so, this sort of thing happens. Maybe that's all it takes for us to forget our evil bent. Our bad potential. To deny our ability to sink. To be slothful. To be apathetic to the will of our leaders.

To not master our own hearts.

But because we are now paying the cost doesn't give us the right to say God is judging mankind.

As far as I'm concerned, we are judging ourselves.

But it does make me wonder about the *final* apocalypse. The end of mankind. Is this the makings? A few governments? A few banks? There seems to be just a few of everything.

Except nightmares. There are plenty of those.

Tonight the wind comes from the darkest corner of ocean; a place in the utter east where sky and water meet. It leans into our sails, pulling our tired ketch northward. We keep our masts upright and I fly just enough canvas to part the bodies. It isn't prudent to sail hull speed. And quickness has no purpose. We have nowhere to go and no place we want to be.

On deck and in the rigging, ice forms as if we were still off Greenland in the Labrador Sea. But those months are gone.

Now we glide in the lee of large icebergs that knock down the waves. We fly with just enough sail to maintain steerage and we come about every other watch. This keeps the spray from forming ice on our deck and keeps us crossing familiar seas.

No one likes to feel thumps in the night or hear the sound of breakers beyond our sight. We have long been in a confused sea beneath pure black skies despite the feeble efforts of the moon. We haven't had a star fix for many seasons. Only a soft, dark shifting glow that lets us know a moon is somewhere beyond.

And we have other reasons for clinging to the icelines.

I think back.

I was there when people started taking sides. Name-calling. Getting lathered in fear. I saw them take control. I saw them punish severely, cruelly. That's the long and short of it.

The inevitable.

And there we were. Nurches. Church Nurches. We were named that because we were separated from The State. We were the ones who encouraged the tolerable to become intolerable.

Some of us called what was happening evil, but that was nothing new. In those days we called everyone and everything evil.

And they were!

They did whatever they wanted; whenever they wanted. And they did it to whomever they wanted to. Entire cities acting like Noah's blood-spilling neighbors.

We said their lust for perfect medicines were poison to the soul because they took away man's common enemy: illness.

"It's not good for people not to have an enemy," my dad had said.

His worry didn't last long.

The fools and their promises. Their mistakes made people worse.

And there we were. A bunch of bad-mouthing, finger-pointing Nurches. Kissing cousins to Nero's Jews!

I guess we had it coming.

We were the League of the Intolerant.

I look up. In front of my helm the shivering boy pulls harder on his blanket as if his shaking can snap off the grip of frost. His face is covered, but I know he can still smell.

Cold seals the scent of decay, only to be thawed within us when we inhale. We try to lock out the stink, or sail beyond its reach, but it follows us like birds tangled in kite string. Over time it sears our sinuses, numbing them from countless mucus cleansings.

I look beyond the boy. I turn to the rigging and see where our frayed halyards along the masts have gathered ice. Beyond the spreaders hang the constellations. I see them on faith and remember how they used to swing in our standing rigging like strings of Christmas lights. That was when the eerie waves still surged and boiled out from under the icebergs and sometimes rolled them over as if they were snowballs on a hill. The waves pitched us to an extent that we had much damage. But we have nothing to whine about compared to the cities that the waves are breaking upon.

I drop my eyes back to the boy.

The only thing any of us know of this young boy is his name.

Jaffnel.

He is staring at me from a crack in the blanket.

He sits up and looks around.

Snakes and Ladders

Jaffnel shivers hard. He always spills his warmed water, but he doesn't flinch when his hand gets wet.

"He will likely die tonight," my mother from down below had said as she took my hand before my watch. "But if something happens, don't trust anything he says. You know I wouldn't."

"Don't worry," my father added. "Where he's at, only a few can return. But if you do appear to him, be leery of what causes him to drift. Would you like some warm drink?"

Jaffnel blinks up the black sacks under his eyes and coughs. He covers his mouth with a glove made from a wool sock that catches the dark snot of infection. His gaunt cheeks look liked stretched-out, deflated balloons as his small mouth comes out from under the blanket. His lips shine in the night with what could be blood.

All we know about Jaffnel is that he is from East America. How he got into the sea is still a mystery. No surprise there. We can't figure out how any of the dead got here. But the floating heads own the horizons, nevertheless.

"Jaffnel is smart. Smart as paint," my father had said after discovering his name in a book kept dry alongside his body. My father took the book. "He used the belts of the dead to rope bloated carcasses into a raft."

I know nothing of the book. Nor does my mother. Only my father. He hasn't spoken of it in days.

It changed him. He hasn't talked but a few sentences since he got a hold of it. He won't let me see it. When he looks at me his eyes move from left to right as if he is still reading the pages.

I know my father found Jaffnel sheltered atop a raft of bodies who had all shaved their heads.

"Around his body were dozens of garbage bags, each twisted to allow dryness and airflow like a Coast Guard Dry Suit," my father had said to me before he read the book. "His little body didn't do the wrapping. He couldn't have!"

Inside the wrappings along Jaffnel's skin was the insulting hair of the bald people who shaved themselves to give his life a chance! There is where we found a journal of sorts! We have news.

But the news changed my father. It didn't add to him. It took away from him. And he had little to give.

We know the dead helped Jaffnel squeeze life from the hypothermic sea. I know he has a story to tell.

Yet I know the stories in the book quieted my father. And stilled him. He now only leaves the cabin for his daytime watch. He won't come up in the dark.

"Jaffnel is close to death this night," my mother had repeated as I prepared for my shift.

She still wants to protect me.

I now look at Jaffnel and remember his fight. I recall how his body shivers away the days and how his teeth rattle him through these few nights he had been with us.

He won't go below. He obsesses with staying topside.

And he is now looking at me from a dark area of the cockpit beyond the red binnacle light. "Delaware is a patriotic state," he whispers.

I jolt.

I look over my shoulder, then I look at his face, well hidden in the shadow below the hood of his blanket.

I look over at the slot in the cockpit where we store the ship's log.

I now see his dark lips move against his white face and the fingers in his sock scratch salt clumps from his scalp.

"Fire truck ladders hooked us atop of those old telephone poles. You know, the ones that used to hang wire? That's where they put most of us. They soaked us in gas and dish-soap and hung us up there with the flags," Jaffnel says, his eyes drifting off to where a horizon should be.

I remember the flags. I hear them ripple and clap in the breeze as they swim in the wind above our town and along our roads.

Flags flew on every old phone pole. Below the blue sky of the entire country they rippled as a tribute to the power of the wind which promised us energy. All rallied to fly flags.

Flags identify and unify.

Then each town started waving its own flags. Its own colors. Each community started whistling their own Dixie, so to say. Calling their own shots. Making their own recipes for their own needs. They tried to keep their own energy. To own their own disasters.

One town even…

I then hear what Jaffnel just said and I stare deep into his face and see his eyes.

They are dark with memory of haunting sadness.

He is gone again.

Maybe for good.

I look away from him. I see our life lines disappear beyond him into the darkness of the foredeck. All is still but the wind in the rigging and the soft hiss of our waterline.

A small berg of ice scraps our hull like iron, and Jaffnel jolts and turns his eyes back to the decking.

We both know better than to stare into the water.

Stretching the cold from my fingers, I feed line into the headsail winch and slow our progress to a crawl as if the spot on the water off our stern had inspired the boy to speak.

Jaffnel's eyes are emptier than an unplugged TV.

I hope he says more for the log, but I don't know why I want this.

Jaffnel sees me again. "Trucks dumped steel rebar rods and they smithed them over loud, blue propane flames and bent them into S-shaped hooks. Meat hooks. Snake hooks. They were heavy, like big crowbars, but sharpened on both ends. Everyone in the crowds carried two hooks and they clanged them as they surrounded the houses. Snakes and ladders." He looks at me confused.

"Ladders and hooks," he whispers. His eyes go blank. "They hooked us through the shoulders or worse. The ends of fire truck ladders hooked the other end of the S-crowbar and up the screaming went. Bad men climbed up the ladders. They unhooked the screaming from the ladders and hooked them to the tops of the poles. After another squirt of gas and soap from the fire hose, the screaming lit up the town."

He wiggles his fingers inside his wool sock as he lowers his hand. "Soap gas and blood drool down." He lifts his hand. "Fire goes up. They burned their flags too."

Jaffnel goes quiet.

Twisting, I turn behind and peer through the darkness off our stern, scanning the horizon for light and noise. No one is out there. I half expected to see the burning dead.

I recall the stars and the moon. Such simple treats. How they laid claim to the beauty of night for eons. But when they got covered by dirt and dust, panic came and hope left. They now shine beyond the layers of black grime above our heads. Only the faint glow hints to the moon above, hindering all sense of direction.

I turn back and face Jaffnel.

He sees me. "Night after night until every old phone pole

became a light pole. And our town still had all its poles. Atop every pole burned one of us. They used us for candles. Like the Romans. They danced all night in the orange glow of torches that spun off funnels of fire. They sang their songs in the aroma of black oil smoke and burning people."

I stare at him.

He lurches and shivers hard.

I see his face beyond the glow of the compass. It shines red because of sweat.

Those fires are scalding his mind.

I see.

It is but one of many sights I have been given. It is but another thousand word image that weighs down our vessel as if trying to break the rhythm of our hull in the rollers.

Jaffnel pulls the blanket over his head and stretches out the lines of frost in the wool.

I wonder if he will survive the night. If he does, I hope he will speak again. This thought disturbs me. I care more for his story than for his life.

4

God's Gallows

The snowflakes are brittle and so dehydrated that they hover above our deck and surf with us as if we had just stirred a hatch of white mosquitoes. When they come near me, I try not to let them land on me. They thaw and release a sharp smell.

Smell makes everything in the past more real.

I look at a corner of the cockpit where a dusting of flakes have found refuge. In the morning when the snow melts, it will be an area of dirt. Many kinds of dust are still in earth's atmosphere.

I think of the martyred professor.

The professor scares me. He makes the hair on my arm feel as if each root has been dipped in ant poison.

I'm talking about my father's friend.

He told me how the world ends. "I hope I'm wrong," he had said. "If I'm right, I'll be the first to go!"

He was right.

They killed him quick.

"Why?" I had asked.

"In an apocalypse you can't have people like me helping people make sense of stuff."

They didn't gaff the professor on a double ended, S-shaped crowbar hook and burn him on an old pole like the Nurches in Jaffnel's state.

We lived in Maine.

Up there they just shot people in the head.

Big hands held my face and made me watch.

I peed my pants as he climbed the slippery mound of

bodies. I cried when they loaded their smoking guns and I again stuck my fingers in my ears.

Before they pulled their triggers, he looked at me and saw the wet spot in my crotch. He nodded.

I felt for the first time that it was normal to watch people die for God and normal to pee on yourself. Maybe they go together. I broke loose, made it home and told my dad.

I still hear our footfalls and feel the cold dew and the scratchiness of the long weeds as we made it to the harbor.

I carried my little sister.

My parents carried my two brothers.

We held our hands over their eyes so they wouldn't see our house spiraling flame high into the night.

Our sail unfurling seemed to squeal in fear as our head-sail rolled out and snapped open. We caught the soft wind of temperature change and ghost-sailed out the channel mere minutes after the professor's death.

Looking back at our fishing village, we sailed through the maze of still windmills. Their huge white wings flickered in the flash of rifle muzzles and the glow of burning buildings.

What sounded like firecrackers is my last memory of town.

An eerie orange glow filled the clouds above our town, giving bright color to our dark wake. Much of the land seemed to be burning.

"Why didn't the professor have a plan?" I had asked my father when we were alone on that first night.

"He did."

"Why didn't he follow it?"

"He did. He saw God's Gallows as his plan."

"Is it a good plan?"

"Yes."

"What about us? Why not us?"

At this my father just gazed out over the dark sea and tightened his hands on the helm. He looked at me. "Was he afraid?"

"No."

"Good."

"What about the Nurches who want to fight?" I had asked, because a bunch of people in our church had houses full of guns.

At this my father smiled. It was a sad smile, just like the professor's.

I clamp my gloved hands to the ship's wheel. Because it is chrome, we covered it with lines of cord to weaken the sting of the frost.

The night air bites my throat.

Off in the dark, a wave thrashes. It isn't a good splash, like the natural boil of a cresting sea.

It is a tail-slap of a predator feeding on the dead sea souls.

5

Spend Your Future

I tap my fingers on the wheel to keep the blood flowing and look east.

"Look to the east," the professor had said. "Always look east for signs of light. Hope comes from the east, not from a beast," he pointed at his TV.

The man who was talking on every channel looked at us. We looked back.

"The simple truth is ugly," the TV man said. "Truth being that it is inhuman to enslave another person in any way. Physical slavery, America abolished long ago, but a new master is over us and his financial, mental, spiritual and medical control makes a cruel combination. We will fight his oppression, people! As we have mentioned before, he wants us to behave like victims. Because a true victim is a great client! A victim can never reach agent status as long as a society of prosperity promotes opportunities for predation!

"SPEND YOUR FUTURE!" He pointed at us with both index fingers from in the TV. "Is the program that provides all who willingly come to take advantage of our technology to equip themselves to become long-term, thinking people? A long-term thinker is an Agent! To be free of burdens financially, physically, spiritually, mentally and sociologically is to brave the hindrances that have historically suppressed our citizen rights! The slave and the master can now embrace equal rights. In us is the opportunity to create a global culture of fairness and unprecedented peace!"

I looked at the professor. "What's he talking about?"

"Here it comes," he said to my father, who sat next to me.

They leaned closer.

I looked at the bowls of chips.

"As I clearly stated before," the TV leader assured us. "Any person using our accounting system, automatically deposits capital into that person's ten accounts. When you spend, you invest at the very least into seven grids. Some common investment choices are healthcare, retirement, home equity, college funds for your children, leisure time investment, healthy living, travel and sponsored giving to charity status groups.

"With our plan, you save as you spend! When you spend, we recycle one percent of every global spent into every category. Eight percent of every global spent is your future. When you SPEND YOUR FUTURE, fairness begins!

"The Network only needs one global for every four you buy. If you need eight, the Network needs two. Those of more prosperity who buy over eight globals will give the Network a little more. But know this! When we come willingly, come openly, come longingly with the hope to SPEND YOUR FUTURE, families will be equipped and equip their offspring! Together we can and must command lifestyles of pure equality! And such equality must be the very pillar of society!"

I looked at my dad.

He looked at the professor.

"What?" I had asked.

The professor muted the TV. "It's all there," my father said.

The professor nodded. "If you save your money, you cannot save your money. It's brilliant."

"So you pay yourself only by spending? It sounds good to me. What's wrong with that?" I had asked.

"Nothing. Or everything" the professor said. "Say a woman wants a Coke to stay awake as she drives her kids back from grandma's."

"Yea," I said.

"But her heath care says she needs to have green tea instead. The network says she can only buy unsweetened green tea. See? Her healthcare and her spending plan co-exist."

That got me thinking. I hate green tea.

My father looked at me. "Thomas Jefferson said that a government big enough to give you everything you need is strong enough to take everything you have."

"So the government took her Coke?" I remember nodding to this.

The two men looked at each other.

"It's the beginning."

"By spending your future, everyone will know whenever you step out of line through accounting."

"It's great to be healthy, but who wants doctors saying Amendment Rights are unhealthy? Saying it's better to breath cold air than to heat your house with a wood stove?"

"Leisure money and travel funds are good, but who really enjoys going to a store where only the suggested shopping list has the greatest discount?"

"It's the brotherhood without being called family. Everybody will love it," the professor said.

The professor was right.

In less than two years he was killed.

We stepped off the grid too.

We went to the sea.

The fears of the ocean were nothing compared to land.

Or so we thought.

6

Hog Pen

The big lady next to the companionway hatch takes warm water with a hint of a flavor from my father, who seems reduced to work the galley. She holds it in front of Jaffnel, who remains still, then leans my way and hands it back to me.

I nod thanks to her, holding my voice because my throat is cold and sore. Like the professor, I try to be brave, but I'm afraid of the water, of freezing to death and other things. I'm afraid of what is in the water feeding on the dead.

"Are you thinking of the professor again? He's so brave," Bethanal says. She is kind and sensitive and likes to listen to me talk of the professor, but she is also talkative.

She lived on a ranch out west and she is fat. Real fat. Fat enough to float in freezing water for a long time without dying.

The cold only shrunk her down a bit.

We used the boom with block and tackle to get her aboard.

She stays in the cockpit because she pukes so much when below. We don't allow her on the foredeck because she has absolutely no balance.

Despite having legs, she's more like a ball. Whenever the wind puffs and we heel, she crashes across the decking like a loose cannon. She could take out a mast.

But she's smart. Smart as white on rice, so she sits down and never moves. She reaches for things by leaning, then leans the other way to pass them on. She has her spot.

Now she's nibbling something hard and leathery, working

it into her warm water to form a tea of some kind. She got that from us.

We are more rodent than human in our eating habits because of the lack of food.

She won't be fat for long.

I don't know her whole story because she always ends up bawling and blowing snot. I know she is from the plains states. Nebraska, maybe. And they had it pretty rough up there after the fires went though. Livestock died within weeks of the barn and crop fires. The roads were down. They weren't ruined. You don't ruin an expressway by burning the grass around it. But you do stop people from driving on them when the bridges are gone.

"We stacked the charred timbers of our church to keep out the wind. It was our mistake," Bethanel says as I finish summarizing Jaffnel's words in the log. She is looking at her tea as if it were communion.

Having the log open with pen in hand seems to invite her testimonial.

I don't want to look at her, but I don't want be mean. I do want to sleep after my shift, and I know she is burdened with bad news of her own. I worry too about Jaffnel.

He doesn't need to hear any more bad things. His blanket isn't soundproof.

My eyes move across her face, then I shift them to study our black headsail.

Hers follow mine.

"Our church was white like a normal sail," she says.

I nod. Hearing about her church isn't bad.

"You know, after it was burned and all was dead and rotted away, a few of us gathered at the holy site." She stares into the waves.

The moon glows through the dirt patch in the sky. It

forms a black-purple light. In this darkness she can still see the floaters making ripples across oily waters as they bob. She stares at the frozen, white faces of the dead.

I can't.

She shudders as the tail of a predator splash sends chilling spray her way. She turns to me, a water droplet is on her wide cheek. "We should've never stacked the timbers."

I sense regret. "It would have happened anyway. You couldn't have prolonged it." I repeat what the professor had said.

"They penned us in with those timbers. Did you know that?" she asks. "It's one thing to be in jail. It's a whole different world when they use holy timbers to pen you into a place!"

I look at the button on the helm. If I push it, a bell sounds in my father's cabin. It might not do anyone any good, but it sends an alarm nevertheless.

I won't push it just for Bethanal.

My father doesn't seem to be ready for more news.

That's why he gives me the nightshift. He won't do the dark with the rescued. "I need to sleep when they are awake," he says.

Mom is changing too. She doesn't let the young ones topside any more, ever. She keeps them in the V birth, with the doors closed. She needs to protect them. She runs her fingers through their hair. She passes the days and nights doing that.

But I'm now drawn to their stories. I look at Bethanal and sense that she feels like talking. "Do you have a story for the logbook?" I ask.

Bob's Hardware

Bethanal touches her fingers and thumbs together and makes a circle with both of her hands. "They used a metal gate post on some of us because the normal fence post couldn't take the heat. Do you understand what I'm talking about?"

I nod as if her story is already in the log. But a part of me hopes she can hold together. I want to hear about it.

She nods too, relieved that she doesn't have to tell me. Or maybe it is the other way around. Maybe now she feels I am in her pain circle and she can confide.

Either way, something changes in the air around her.

It comes between us and takes my focus off the helm. In silence it taunts me. It reminds me of who I am and what is happening. It tells me that there is nowhere to hide.

It wants my hope.

It wants to kill it.

"They were saving me for something special. But they never got me, did they?" she exhales a smile. It didn't stay long. She leans toward me. Her face shines red in the binnacle light. It glows as if dipped in black blood.

She holds up all her chubby fingers to me and then she bends her thumbs down in front of her dark, googly-like eyes. "It took them eight hours to cook my mother," she nods this to me then holds up a hand like a hatchet. "They gutted her like a fish and gave her innards to be slurped up by some hogs in the next pen over; the room where Mrs. Visser once taught 5th Grade Sunday School."

Bethnal lifts a hand above her head and holds an

unseen necktie. Then she yanks her head crooked, rolls her eyes back and hangs out a thick tongue. She retracts her tongue, straightens her neck and leans to me. "The same room where Widow James hung herself the week before. She stretched her own neck." Bethanel shakes her head back and looks at me. "Will Widow James still go to heaven?"

I shrug. I look at the warning bell.

She lowers her hand and leans in. She unscrews something in the air between us and pours it onto the binnacle, then her hand spreads and massages the area and starts stroking side to side. "They used paint brushes from Bob's Hardware to spread the barbecue sauce. My mom was slow roasted and after all the spices, the whole town could smell it and everybody came. They carried their own plates and knives. Children too."

Bethanal's right hand turns in the air, motioning how meat gets roasted rotisserie style over fire. She looks at me as if she is going to offer me a chocolate. "A lot of people were already there. They stayed during the cooking because those who took turns cranking the skewer got to pull pieces off so mom didn't get overcooked."

I look to the east.

It is as dark as the west.

I turn back to Bethanal.

Her cheeks are thick and wide on her glistening face. Short hair covers her huge head. Tears as big as marbles form and roll down.

"Nothing went to waste," she says. "They picked her clean. Then they fed her bones to the hogs and I listened to the piggies crunch on them for hours."

She pauses and then concludes a fact with a furrow of her chin. "Hearing my mom's bones getting grounded up and swallowed by hogs was worse than watching the town cook and eat her." Bethanal puts her hands on her face.

She starts one of her blubbering gushers that has the potential to wake up the little ones and frazzle my mother all the more.

But she cuts it off and looks at me. "Do you wanna know the worst of it?"

I hold still.

She leans even closer to me. "I wanted to eat some of my mom so bad. I've never been so hungry as I was back then. They cooked off us church members to feed the town. Can I have some of your water?"

I hand it to her.

"Then he made a law that they couldn't do that anymore. He's a good man. He saved me!" Her eyes flare and she nods her head. "They never got to eat me, did they?" she now shakes her head.

Her voice drains of energy as she stares across the eel-infested North Atlantic and then she looks back at me. "And here I am."

Eworld and Easy Pickings

The forward watch creeps out from darkness of the foredeck, grasping the rigging with one hand and cradling the other. He is held fast by a life harness with its strong line and clip. As he makes his way back, he goes slow, not because the topsides are icy and he has to stage his clip. He isn't slow because of his injured, blood-oozing right hand.

He is certain of each step because of the water. He goes slow out of great respect for the sea.

We all respect the water. More accurately, what's in the water.

Not that either has any respect for us.

He comes back but his watch isn't over.

My father doesn't want him around me, but he has never come out and said it. Nor does he have the will to enforce it. He has his own problems now.

I felt it only once when dad interrupted him. "More water?" my dad had asked when the man started to talk about land.

His name is Timmons and he makes into the cockpit. He holds himself steady and keeps his wits as the boat adjusts to a rogue roller. His face is strained with pain lines because his injured hand is below his heart and pulsing. He stays as close to the middle of the ship as possible.

I can tell by the way he shifts his body that he is ready to get out of the frigid wind and have his warm water. I hand him the thermos.

Timmons seems to know things about sea life and animals in general.

I don't know how I surmised that. Maybe I overheard my father and the professor talking about people like him.

What people like Timmons have done has played a huge role in the unraveling.

Timmons is a scientist.

I think of the professor.

He often spoke of science. "Life is a train wreck speeding away from the big apple," the professor had said, "A scientist on a power trip wants more and more of Adam's apples. It's Adam and Eve surfing their endorphin rush. Genetics! Playing God and torturing creation. Then and now. At the beginning and at the end!"

Timmons looks at the big girl sobbing, but he knows better than to reach out and comfort her. People don't touch each other anymore. Getting touched makes their nerves remember the evil world where heartless people do heartless things.

Timmons looks at me and we nod. He wears a sleeping bag like a dress, with three holes cut in for his head and arms. He brushes off ice crystals and sits.

It's waterproof and warm.

We found him in the sea in his bag, floating like a worm in a cocoon.

He had cut the holes after he boarded.

Timmons is a survivor. One who can read the weather. Interpret the writing on the wall. Fear the beat of dangerous drummers.

Pretty much anybody still alive falls into one of these groups.

The dumb are dead, dirt, dinner, debris and dust.

"You know where we're going, don't you?" Timmons asks.

I see ooze where a finger used to be. It's missing because

his gizmo, I think. *I'm not going to ask.*

Don't have to. It's overboard now.

Everybody got them. They were rewards to citizens of privilege in countries of promise. They were for those who had nothing to hide. Packaged with incentives, allowing their owners to think long-term. The future of share our wealth. They were the center of the financial health and wealth building plan, SPEND YOUR FUTURE.

Of course they came when health threats were making people freak. They came to help superstores stop spreading diseases.

They came when we became a people who couldn't share.

I remember days when we handed credit cards back and forth and even real money.

How stupid is that?

Viral Terrorists and Fear Mongers had easy pickings.

The piercing that was done to Timmons, and to most everybody else, sure took care of that problem.

No more contact.

No more stealing.

No more thieves.

No more money exchange.

EWorld. Where honest people are kept honest!

I remember the commercials.

We refused to get it done to us. Some Nurches did, but not us. Drop a knee to show allegiance and to activate the thing?

Yea.

Right.

We Nurches just went hungry as we wasted hours and then days waiting in the few cash-only lines. Then the few credit card only stores. Then the final store. The back street trucks.

I remember the waiting to be the hardest.

People don't like to wait.

The plastic windshield in front of us, called a dodger, shelters us from the wind and water. It collects ice. Timmons taps it and particles clink off and land in piles along the gunnels.

Bethanal jumps.

Jaffnel twitches and a light dusting of snow falls off his blanket.

Tonight is a gentle sea. We have been combing the lee of this iceberg for a month now. We need the rest and good water.

We know the calm can't last forever, and we watch the horizons for movement. We only have a few moments to put the bow of Defiance into the rogue rollers when they come.

But now all is black.

We keep sail reduced and our pace to a crawl.

Most of the time we barely feel the tidals because we are well off the continental shelf and deep in the North Atlantic where it is still safe. But the earth has been alive for years and whenever two rogues collide, the water becomes dangerous.

"Oceanfront living used to be a luxury. People wanted it. Imagine that!" My father had said once.

When I think about people wanting to live by the water, it sounds like Dumb calling Stupid, a Moron.

Timmons rubs the wrist above the wound and looks at the closed companionway door. He is from the desert regions of the southwest. Arizona, maybe.

And even though a lot of people live and love the deserts, none of them ever seemed to care about what the scientists actually built out there under the hot sand. Until it was too late.

I watch Timmons shuffle in a circle like a scratching kitten as he prepares to sit.

He decides to stay on the other side of the cockpit from Jaffnel and Bethanal. He sits and looks at me.

I nod to him. "What's some of the creepy things you made out there in the desert, Timmons?" I ask. I couldn't help it.

He smiles and snorts, then his eyes go sad in the red light of the compass.

"Your dad will kill me."

"You mean the cook?" Bethanal asks.

"It's for the log. We need all the stories."

"What we did isn't for no storybook. Not even one for Helen Keller."

"What?"

"With no gene patent laws? We did whatever we wanted," he says. "Making public the G-16 gene patents was the only thing he did right. Too bad he opened them all the way. But I guess it was only a matter of time. And with all the things changing, change had to be done to the box as well."

I shiver beneath fleece and gortex despite being warm and dry.

Timmons is going to talk and my father isn't up to stop him.

Wind swirls snow out of the corners.

"What have I done?" he asks somberly as he watches me and my logbook.

I finish recording Bethanal's story and close the ship's log. I am going to have to summarize Timmons. I know that already.

Timmons is looking at his hand as if it is was oozing something besides infection.

Darwinian War

Bethanal looks at me and I see her shake her head in the darkness. She holds out her hand and I see it shaking even before Timmons speaks. She doesn't want to be around Timmons, but she doesn't have the balance to leave the cockpit. Not when it's this dark. She pulls her shaking hand back under the blanket as if it were the head of a turtle.

"Our boss loved new mods. We had twenty on my team, and our company had about seventy teams. The deserts had three thousand companies for a while, most of them bigger than us. They thought they were safe because they kept us in the desert. If that isn't botanist calling the biologist green!"

I look away into the rolling darkness of the waves, nervous about not having a bow watch.

His story is coming. People like him started the Darwinian War. Survival of the fittest. Where the strong ate the weak. Only their strong ate everything.

"Have you ever heard of the word ecosystem?" Timmons asks.

I search my brain, but recall nothing. "Is that where all animals lived together?"

"Basically," he says and looks over the water, where a tail slaps the surface, sending out circles of ripples. Something lifts a body and then plunges it under the water. More circles.

"Have you ever seen one?" I ask.

"Of course."

"What's it like?"

"Fragile," he says.

I snort air out of my nose.

Fragile was something that got killed long ago.

"I remember catching bugs in my yard," I say.

He smiles.

"Bugs are now ninety-nine percent of the life mass on the planet."

"Who made them?" I nod to the water.

"Did you know the oceans used to feed much of the planet?" he asks. "Now the planet just feeds them," he looks to the sea and my eyes follow his. We see some S-patterns skimming the surface of the dark, oily purple water that has a phosphorescence glow when not in the glow of the moon-clouds.

"I hate them," I say.

"They don't need to eat but once a year. If that. Did you know they can cannibalize each other and not die? They were engineered that way. ET's made them."

"Extra Terrestrials?" Bethanal asks me.

"Eco Terrorists. They were from a Dutch group, they say. At least they were the ones they caught and punished. But they're not to blame. There's a part of all of us who wanted to do it. To be the one to do it."

"Do what?"

"Crash it."

"Crash what?"

"Life."

"Why?"

"I think it's our nature. I think it's what we like to do when we are less than ourselves. Our bent to control and limit the simplest of things. Things like food."

"That's awful," Bethanal says.

"Awe and pride are the same."

"Why then does the professor say that every mutation

results in a weaker creature?" I ask.

"Because it's true. You think you can breed poodles together and get a wolf? But we're not talking about mutations, are we? Genetic Terror doesn't come from mutations. Terror comes from someone's mind!"

"So an Eco Terrorist is a Genetic Terrorist?"

"In our case. They were spreading out military and agriculture contracts on this stuff like butter before Wisconsinites when peace threatened. And once we started looking into that corner of Mr. Potato's Head, a lot of fries came into the grinder. Genetics! You learn to love it! You create the curse that keeps on cursing."

We say nothing for a long time.

No one does.

Or can.

We just remember the times when things used to be. We let our memories out and we see animals in our minds. Thousands of them. We saw them mainly on TV, but we see them nevertheless.

"Butter sounds nice," Bethanal says.

I shake my head and blink away the sting of the salt breeze. A tear chills my cheek and I leave it alone. I keep heading south, hugging the lee of the berg, keeping a mile or so off it. I know I have no bow watch to guide me around body clusters or smaller icebergs, so I tack off the wind to view some of the darkness before I sail over it. I let sail out and slow Defiance just above steerage, not having energy to command Timmons to go back to the foredeck.

Body clusters are more dangerous to us than icebergs. It is where eels hatch and die. When the dead eels cluster, they bloat and release their toxins of oil and gas to ward predators. As if they still had to worry about that.

Timmons smiles. "The Dutch were brilliant. You have to

say that. The DNA in every cell is coated with Anoxellan. Absolutely no part of the eel promotes life. Eighteen months. Did you know that? The Darwinian War started and ended in 18 months. Almost every creature on land and water is gone. Except us, of course. And birds. But we won't last long. Not against them. They love to eat and eat to love. And no one can eat or even touch them without this." He lifts his hand from the round puddle of puss by the winch where it was oozing.

"What's Anoxellan?"

"Anoxellan is a French kissing cousin of Anthrax."

"What's that?"

"Another poison. Nearly harmless by comparison. How long you been at sea?"

I shrug my shoulders.

He won't believe me anyway.

"Do you know you're the only family I've seen in ten years?" Timmons says.

I smile, thinking of my two sleeping brothers and my little sister. We are a gaunt, ragged, salt-crusted and scurvy-fighting family, but we're a family, nevertheless.

"I can't believe you still have food," he says

Bethanal puffs her breath.

"Not much," I say.

"How did you know?"

"Barrels were cheap," I say. "So my dad filled them with whatever."

"But dog food?" Bethanal says.

"The last ones. Yes," I say. "That's all there was. But he didn't think it would really happen and we always had dogs around."

"He thought ahead more than any other person I've ever heard of." Timmons tone shuts up Bethanal, piddling over the quality of her survival.

"Did you really cut off your own finger?" I ask, recalling the screams on the foredeck the day we fetched Timmons from the water.

"I didn't have a choice. One of them nipped me and the Anoxellan is in the bacteria in their teeth. Kind of like Salmonella."

"I remember hearing you yell."

"You want me to cut off your finger?" he smiles. "Have you ever heard of the Seminole Project?"

"Oh," I say. I was saddened to hear him say this because it is old news. It is nothing good enough for the log.

"That's where it came from," Timmons says. "That was the beginning of the end of ecosystem."

"I thought one of us did that?"

"Surely you didn't learn that from your professor."

"No. But everybody…"

"Who is everybody?" he asks.

I look at him as our vessel rises high atop an enormous swell and we wait until it passes underneath.

"That one's a killer," Timmons says, then looks at me. "Everybody is Them. The same Them who put Him in power. The same Them who issued Spend Your Future? Ticket To Ride? The Rite of Passage. The Cities of Light! The same Them who torched the tarred on the sticks from Rome to Avalon?"

"History repeats itself," Bethanal says.

A blanket rustles and Jaffnel's face is out. His sunken eyes rest equally on all three of us. "You're very close, Bethanal, but evil doesn't repeat. Evil is the constant."

10

Seminole Project

I don't know why I ask Timmons about his genetics. I don't know what's wrong with my innards, but when I think what a scientist can actually make, I see it as very interesting. I say that it is for the log. I say I need to store news for the future. That I need to trap these events like rings in a tree or an air bubble in a glacier for others to discover. But the truth is ever since I read Frankenstein, I've been drawn to the weird stuff really smart people can create. Maybe I just like to roll in the vomit like the Bible-dogs and not be lifted from the muck like God did Adam. Maybe I am drawn to the creators who only play God. Maybe I'm sick.

"Fight your heart. Master your curiosity," my father had said when I kept asking him about the happenings across our land. Back when land was close enough to my memory that I could point west and visualize it just beyond the Elmherst family farm.

"What if I can't?" I had asked that just months into our escape.

He went below and returned with a book, Heart of Darkness.

"A book? None of my friends read books."

"Look around," he had pointed across the waters. "How many friends do you see?"

I now turn back from the black waters and look at Timmons. "What's the Seminole Project, Timmons?" I ask. Maybe he'll say something new.

Bethanal shakes her head slow, warning me.

How come she knows?

"They say it was those Boa snakes that got loose in the Florida Everglades after Hurricane Andrew, the storm that put the first pin-prick in our system. They say those pet snakes that got lose back then inspired it. Or were they Burmese Pythons? Whatever. In a few decades that snake conquers the ecosystem. They ate the alligators, for Jeeper's Creep! And more than a few people too! Sure, most of them were kids, but they still got swallowed whole. And the snakes did it naturally. They were hunted, but the snakes used our natural resources against us. It's a big swamp down there. It was a simple, non-indigenous snake that people once sold for pets that changed it all. Forever."

I look around. Nothing new so far, except that Timmons knows history.

"Changed the world forever," he added.

Bethanal and I turn and face him.

"Remember the old movies where giant things ate screaming people?" he asks.

I stand and peer forward as Timmons talks. I'm worried about the darkness beyond the bow.

Timmons is leaning against the mizzen mast, looking east.

It is still black in the east.

"Remember when stars pierced the night mere degrees above the waves?" he asks.

The mizzen hums and I turn to port to spill the freshening breeze. The mainsail is down and lashed with lines. We save it for emergencies. A small headsail hangs on the forestay.

"What's land like now?" I ask.

"People are crying out like the teacher said they would," Bethanal says, her eyes are as void as her voice. "They are crying out for God to bring down the mountains and crush them. They want the Bible prophecies!"

I look at her, then at Timmons, and shake my head, hoping that he does too.

He doesn't.

"What? I pray that," Bethanal says.

Timmons bows his head. "The highways were once lined with marching people. The hopeful. They can't be stopped or turned away," Timmons says. "My generation might be the last after all. But we are still walkers on the Highway of Hope."

"Every generation thinks it is the last. That it can't get worse. The professor said so," I say.

"We were granted safe passage once on the highways," Timmons says. "But it wasn't Gandhi's walk to the sea. It was a safe passage only from people."

"The Highway to Hope is for the terrorists. We are terrorists," Bethanal points at me and nods like the teacher she is.

"Why go?" I ask, as if my family is the pillar of proper homesteading.

"Have you ever seen a Seminole? Or someone get crushed by one?" Timmons asks. "Or walked through the fields of crystallized human bone snake excrement?"

I look at my feet. Just sailing through hundreds of thousands of drowned and frozen dead doesn't qualify me to ponder the horror of land. I am on the outside of disturbia.

I am protected.

I look at my feet. I know I won't be on the outside for long.

Timmons had more to say.

11

Ticket To Ride

Bethanal sits in front of me, propped up under the dodger. Timmons is behind. I can't see both at the same glance. They come at me in stereo.

"We, all of the shamed, we were all given a Ticket to Ride," Bethanal says. "So we rode."

"What?" I ask.

Timmons adjusts what was left of his hand and grits his teeth.

I wait for the pain to pass from his face.

"The tickets are for terrorist," he says. "No one's at war against any one faith. But all are at war with the intolerants within every faith. So anyone with a bone to pick with another could go to the highways to escape the horror. Then we get ticketed to Greenzone," Timmons says.

I nod. Why didn't he just say so? I open the log.

"The Greenzone Ticket," Timmons summarizes with empty eyes, "is the one way ride to where rescue from the frozen sea is a shrunken family on a tiny boat."

I don't think he is very proud of himself. I look overboard at two frosty faces and put the pen to my mouth to thaw the ink in the tip. "So these…"

"Yes," Bethanal says. "The dead among us were granted a Ticket to Ride."

"The eels will have them all gone in a few days," Timmons says.

"But more will come. More are always coming," Bethanal says.

"Why?" I ask.

"Greenzone is where it's safe from the Seminole Project. It's the only place for those shunned by the Cities of Light," Bethanal says.

"Ichabod doesn't use his headless horseman to scare people out of their Sleepy Blue Hollows. He simply puts Seminoles in woods, into the lovely woods, dark and deep. No Young Goodman Brown in his right mind wants to walk by those woods. We are all frightened nobodies running from nobody's too. Don't forget that Death isn't kindly, when it kindly stops for you," Timmons monologues.

I open the log.

This is news, but I still don't understand.

"I don't get it," I say.

"Talk normal," Bethanal asks Timmons.

Timmons exhales. "Take the growth hormone gene that makes something grow fast and fuse it into something that already grows big. Seminoles became reproducible with reproducible results. Then take a docile, organic poison like Anoxellan and splice it into the snakes' DNA at the cellular level. The snakes are toxic to the core just like these eels who own the seas," he nods overboard. "Seminoles own the continent, the eels own the seas. The Snakes of Satan have been loosed," Timmons says.

"Shoot 'em," I say.

"How does one do that, exactly, in a world with no bullets? Besides, they are cold blooded. No infrared or heat sensors work when the creature assumes the temperature to the ground under it. They slither into small spaces and between bars. They were in their third generation before they even made the news. The war was over before it began!"

Bethanal holds out two fingers and drums them in the air like a runner. "He told those southerners to evacuate," Bethanal says. "He praised the Seminoles because they herded people away from the coasts; away from the storms and danger. Us northerners knew."

"He likes his snakes. He likes their purpose," Timmons says. "It was planned before our time. We raced so fast to see the finish line that we didn't know it was just a cliff!"

"What cliff?" I ask.

"Their blood is coated with the antifreeze gene from an Alaskan fish. Like we did with tomatoes so they could grow in Montana a long time ago. Cold can't stop the snakes. Nor the deserts. They burrow. They own the trees of the forest and the sewers of the cities. They can den where the air pools under the ice and in snowdrifts. They swallow us whole, splintering our bones at six-thousand pounds of pressure per square inch. They see in the dark. Forked tongues taste food miles away. They feel the vibrations of our tiptoes. The Seminole Project is the apex of the Darwinian War. Food chains. Animal kingdoms. Ecosystems. All gone. And they can survive like the sea eels. They can eat their own," Timmons turns away and looks in the water.

Bethanal looks at me.

I see her move in the darkness.

She is petting the air as if a cat was in front of her. "He likes them," she says, "The leader who dooms us all likes them."

I look back at Timmons and then at the rescue life ring on the stanchion. I think he's going to jump.

Instead, he takes off his sock he is using as a glove. It is wet with infection and he wrings out and watches it drip down in the scupper. He stands and I see where the deck is dark red in slime from his hand. He pulls a bottle of what looks like whiskey from his pocket and pops the cork with his teeth. He keeps it in his teeth, winces and grunts as he douses his nub hand with his medicine. Then he sits.

I see beads of sweat on his forehead. Ice melts in his eyebrows.

Too weak to sit and hold body form, he looks at me. "Me and the Dutch are the same. We killed the creation of God," he whispers. "Pen that in your Puke Book."

I turn and look into the dark sea, eyes straining for shades of white ice. Shadows of anything. I listen for breaking waves that show me where the icebergs are. I see a few sleepers, but nothing to warrant a change of course.

Only then do I try to imagine what it must be like to be on land. To be among the slithering. Where prowlers, stalkers, ambushers outnumber people. To be where no place is safe. To be where they slide alongside the edges of roads and circle towns at night, seeking access. To be where lone farmers did their best to board up their farmhouses and watch the canned jars of preserves melt away in time.

The puzzle pieces are no longer puzzling. I see why they burned the foliage of continents. I see a world with so many wars on so many fronts.

Timmons grunts, stands and gazes at the foredeck. "I'm going back to my post now. I like the breeze. It's the only thing left on earth that we can't kill," he says.

Bethanal rolls to the starboard gunnel, gags for a moment, then barfs up her water and dog food morsels into the scupper along the gunnels.

She'll be hungry soon.

12

City of Light

The clouds capture a thin circle of dark red glow from the moon. The lunar phase might be weaning. Or waxing. Sometimes the spot is orange. Now it is a blackish red. There was a time when the moon gave light.

A wave boils and turns the water to greasy blood. But the weak albedo only reaches so far. Maybe its for the best. In the east no color shines back from the darkness. The light of the next sunrise is stuck in absorbent black ash.

I wonder what happened to make the air so thick with dust. Then I remember their words.

Bethanal says the country was burned.

Jaffnel speaks of fires.

Timmons tells of animals that needed to be purged by fire.

I remember my village and how its churches flickered fire against the sky like candles when they were burned.

But in all those things, man played a hand. And I do know enough about mankind to make a point. In the end of time, man will play a role.

But God Almighty will deal the deeds.

I see a dull pinkish heap ahead in the darkness. The roar of surf is upon it and Timmons stands and looks back to make sure of a course change.

I turn Defiance to the starboard, allowing more wind to catch sail. She lays over a few degrees and gains a knot. Speed is good when rounding under ice. Steerage is a must.

We sail by as if on tar. The shadow tint of eerie moonlight

shows dirty snow like piles along Maine roadsides in spring-time. The ice collects what has fallen back to earth. But what looks like debris is scattered atop a flattened area.

I lift night vision binoculars and confirm skeletons atop the iceberg. Our presence lifts a small colony of sea birds from their bone pile and they scream warning, as if we were new to their planet.

I think of the professor.

"Those will be modern-day castles indifferent to the help-lessness beyond their gates," the teacher had told my father when Congress proposed moving people into fabricated, green-energy-independent, healthcare communities called Cities of Light.

We were frightened by this news. We liked our town by the Atlantic. My mother and father were at the table. Other friends were there. I stayed around the corner.

My father motioned me over.

"What's happening?" I had asked.

The professor handed me the book, "The Mask of the Red Death".

"Edgar Allen Poe?" I asked.

"This is what's happening," he said. "It's hard to come up with an original idea."

I thumbed the pages and smiled because it was a short book.

The man frowned. He seemed to know what I thought.

"How will they convince us to leave our homes and build theirs?" my father had asked.

I leaned forward.

"I don't know," the teacher said. "It could be something simple, like another bad storm. Something that could make the people balk at another bailout." He drummed his fingers. "Towns like ours are one Nor'easter from being declared another Abandoned Zone. Or it could be that the scientists have really done something they shouldn't have. But more than likely it will be something new. Something no one can see coming."

"Do you think they already know what it is?" another man asked.

"Yes. Too many things are in motion. The catalyst is out there."

"What will it be?" another had asked. We all looked to the professor.

He shook his head. He didn't know.

They left him and went on talking over by the TV.

I kept my eyes on the teacher.

He looked at me and gave his soft smile, and just for a moment I knew he knew. He was already mourning.

Later that week, Nurches again crowded our house. We sensed something like marmites before avalanches. And we somehow knew that our church wasn't sanctuary.

But when the others had all turned away and started talking among themselves, I sat and waited for the teacher to come.

The emergency sirens rang later that night and we were all driven to our televisions to hear the President. He was on every channel again. Something is scary when the channels all show the same news. When the people all look in the same direction. He appeared stoic and unafraid, but the President's hands shook as he reached for the podium.

He looked into the cameras. It was a bad moment. Dozens of microphones were in front of him. He was in the Oval Office. "Our efforts to protect citizens from the fundamental terrorists have failed."

13

Fundamental Terrorism

I wanted to ask but didn't want to get shushed. I felt them crowd around me and peer at the TV. I wanted to leave, but I couldn't without being in someone's way. I then knew the real reason I wanted to go. The answers to all our questions were coming!

"Fundamental Terrorists," the President said, "or FT's, have proven more defiant to our advances in medicine and technology and now they are in possession of a horrible weapon of terror. Just yesterday it was sanctioned by Vatican Island and endorsed by the religious leaders of Africa, South America and some Middle Eastern countries. Their support, establishes each of those groups as Aiders and Abettors to terrorism, and they have made it known to our societies of peace that they are a clear and present danger!" He took a deep breath and a hard look at us, then he inhaled.

"They arrested the Pope?" I had asked.

"Shhh!" a few adults growled.

"I personally ordered, with the support of our Global-Five partners, an emergency shutdown of the World Wide Web. It will be closed for three days. During this time, which will cost our world economy an estimated one trillion in currency globals, the Internet will be purged of the FT bomb recipe. We must find and destroy all Puff Bombs, seek out how they are built, and, more importantly, we must subdue those who build them! We must! We will survive this attack!"

The president took a deep breath. "FT's want to destroy us! They want to attack our electricity. I now invoke STABLE. The Social Turmoil Activation of Brotherhood and Law

Enforcement. Each law enforcement agent will be alongside their cross-trained and deputized government parolees. These brave teachers, post office workers, roadside repairmen and the other subsidized groups will help us acquire and destroy FT weapons. And each town that exposes and apprehends its Terror Cells will be credited one million globals."

I looked at my father.

His fingers were rubbing his whiskers.

I turned to the TV and watched the President rise and go to a computer and sit with two generals who had their hands on their pistols.

The President took out an envelope, slit the seal with a knife and retrieved the card. He typed in a command then extended his index finger and pushed a button.

Probably the enter button, I thought.

My sister came in from the other room. "We were watching the president on the computer and now it don't work," she had said. "Can you come and fix it?"

"Now it doesn't work," my father had said. He looked at me after she left. "It's happening."

The doorbell rang and many in the room jumped. It was the professor from our church. He was sweating. He and my father closed the doors. They let me stay with them as the others watched the spin people explain the president's message on the TV in the other room.

"What are they saying?" I had asked. We were still by the front door.

"They're saying that churches are distributing how to build crude but very effective EMP's," my father had said. "The things from the movies that kill electricity and computer chips," he said to me as if I was stupid. He looked at the professor. "Come on! Can they really be built in a basement?"

I looked at the TV and the spin guys were asking the same

thing.

"Does it matter?" the professor had asked. "The mobs had just been given the authority to arrest us! It just happened. In three days we will learn if the Rapture of God will come before the Great Tribulation!"

"Are you sure?" my father had asked.

The teacher sat down. He sat hard. His eyes emptied of color and focus. He talked to himself. "With no electricity, everyone will be afraid. And everyone will act upon their fear. And in the darkness. . . . It's brilliant in its simplicity. No one will be to blame because the masses cannot see. Even the will of agenda media, bent with greed and power, will be limited. No one will have time to care if it's us or them. "He looked up to us. "The predators will first destroy fundamentalist. Then they will consume each other."

As he spoke, the lights and TV went dead.

Darkness fell.

14

Plymouth Rock

I didn't know what total darkness was until then. Our town became a shadow on the face of a dark land. Our eyes adjusted in the next few minutes and we could make out shapes in our house.

"Electricity has just become a thing of the past," the professor said.

Someone lit a candle and my father returned with a shotgun and a box of shells. He thumbed cartridges into the long chamber under the barrel.

"What is that for, Peter?"

It was the first time I had heard the professor mention my father's name.

"What do you think?"

"If we kill we will be like the heathen," the teacher said.

My father clutched the weapon and finished loading it. He racked one into the firing chamber and loaded another into the breach to fill the last gap.

Someone was going to die.

"It's self defense," my father said.

Go Dad!

"Peter, do not be pagan. If you stop a beating heart, you kill a creation of God."

"Then what am I supposed to do?"

"Stand. Stand beside all the great men before you."

I remember looking around. That didn't sound too healthy.

My mother came in with another candle and doubled the light in the room, showing the wrinkles in faces. Her hand shook, spilling wax, and she moved about like a shadow as she walked.

"But the law is on my side!" my father had said.

The professor laid a hand on his shoulder. "Weren't you listening to the President? He just declared that all Nurch goers are terrorists. The law of the land is now our greatest enemy. Persecution has just been primed."

The room where we sat became brighter as orange flames a half mile away rose above the rooftops.

No sirens sounded.

Shouting voices drifted into our home as people gathered at a blazing church.

I saw the professor's face go grave. I heard footsteps, but I couldn't even hear a car engine.

"It's begun," he had said. "After three days of this, nothing will be left."

"What are you thinking about?" Jaffnel asks me. His head must have been out the blanket for some time. His breath fogs up cold mist before his face, then it is blown away.

I turn my eyes from the indifferent, black eastern sky and look at the boy. "Why didn't you go to a City of Light?" I ask.

"Heaven is the only City of Light," he says.

"Your parents think that?"

"Yes. Even Winthrop had it wrong."

I nod, not having a clue who Winthrop was. "Is that why they went to the tracks?"

"We had to leave."

"Where were you going?"

"To the tracks," he says.

"After the tracks?"

"To the ships."

"After the ships? Where were the ships going?" I ask, and

Jaffnel looks at me.

No answer to that question has yet come my way.

"As a snake was crushing my mother, she yelled, 'Plymouth Rock!'" Jaffnel says. "Plymouth Rock is…" he pulls the covers over his head.

"What happened?" I ask.

The blanket is still.

Bethanal leans forward. "You really don't know? How long have you been on this boat?" Her right hand started mixing the air. Her left levitated back and forth

I shrug.

"Super Storms. Super snakes. Super cities. But the Cities of Light are filled up and walled in." She shapes a box in the air.

Jaffnel moves under his blanket. "Brave New Worlds are for cowards," he says from underneath.

I click the pen and log the odd facts.

Why would thousands of Nurches board vessels promising to take them to Plymouth Rock? Why would they risk going near the coastlines when storms wreak havoc? And snakes abound?

It only takes a few sentences. It doesn't make any sense.

I close the book and look at the black water going by our hull.

A few eels are stroking alongside. They are curious like dolphins used to be.

Maybe they are just hungry.

Maybe we are out of the Dead Sea Souls.

Maybe they want us next.

15

The Life Jacket Man

The companion hatch slides open and the odd-looking man climbs out, steps into the night and sits down next to Bethanal. He hands me warm water with something brown in it. "From the Galleyman," he says.

I nod.

Bethanal looks for her share then turns to mine.

"Mind if I borrow some of your fine internal heat?" he asks her. His strange voice distresses, as if it had to swim through dark air.

"Who are you?" Bethanal asks.

"My name is H. Pompson of Liverpool, my fairsome lady."

"Ah…the sleeper. I thought you died," she says.

"No such luck on both our behalves," he smiles.

"Were we on the same load?" Bethanal asks. She opens her blanket and lets the man merge into her folds.

"Lord, deary, how could that be? You're a Yank by blood, bone and bust! And I thank the Good Lord that you're a combustionable one at that!"

Now I remember.

H. Pompson came aboard when Defiance raised a day-light dump. My father had stopped me from seeing the Dead Sea Souls in daylight. That's what my mother used to call it, back when she could talk about it.

"I need to save you from seeing that," he used to say. Who would have thought that it would cost him his energy to enforce it?

I fear the pressure it put on his mind.

I know my siblings can see up through the hatch and blink at the square patch of orange sky filled with birds. They see fat, white sea birds that carry strings of flesh in their beaks.

But my mother is there to comb her fingers through their hair and hold them.

Of late, I think they are holding her. I look at the logbook and wonder if my father had entered any of this man's records.

I see the entry. It doesn't have a name.

"And what might your name be, my large lady, and how did you find yourself to be a bobbing buoy of heat in this here sea of ice? And a fine buoy you make!" The funnyman says and smiles as he snuggles.

"You can laugh, but this buoy is alive in a sea of dead. Alive in Christ and dead to sin. I'm that in the world's darkest hour, I might add!" Bethanal says. She seems proud enough.

"Stunning. A candle on the water. A lighthouse above the rocks of sin! An igloo on a glacier! Marvelous!"

"And you? You're nothing special. How did you come to be with us? How did you stay alive?" Bethanal asks.

"They fetched me, my dear. Fetched me from the belly of the beast like our good Lord did Jonah."

"You were in the water? How did you survive the cold?" Bethanal asks.

"Like any descent Englishmen, I did." He reached inside his vest and pulled out a stainless flask and shook it. "England's finest. I pickled my blood, my good lady. Desperate times. Desperate times."

I look at the log and read what my father wrote. "Are you the life jacket man?" I ask.

He looks at me. "That I am, my captain. But my whiskey

story sounds more dashing, don't you say? And what might your name be?"

"First Mate," I say, keeping professional distance.

"Quite right. I thank ye and your fine vessel for tipping my gravestone when I was preparing for my Master."

"You believe in The Maker and you're not an American?" Bethanal asks.

"An American? Lordy no. And an Englishman in Heaven? Only a Yank could ask such a boggle. My name is H. Pompson and see me as a Liverpool onion through and through. Bugger being there with no spark, I might add."

"Are you alone now?" Bethanal asks.

The light went out of him then and there. He just lay next to her rolls and she put her meat hook arm over his shoulders.

I don't know what he lost, but I know it was beautiful and I know he lost it in a horrible way.

16

Vlad the Impaler

H. Pompson suddenly lurches to the side of the vessel and thrusts his head over the gunnels, wiggling hard. The rest of him might have momentumed himself overboard if it were not for the heroics of Bethanal.

She grabs him good and rolls her weight on him.

He wretches something fierce and the eels of the deep circle his vomit, opening their mouths and showing rows of curved teeth as they net up the mucus trails. He lunges again as if drawn to their needle-like teeth and Bethanal screams in grit as she clamps to him.

The sheer size of Bethanal holds him fast and he comes to.

He screams just once, then relaxes and Bethanal thrusts his body to where her space is and she slams herself next to him.

The cockpit is still.

He lays fetal.

Bethanal is sweating. Her arms are out like a Sumo and she is ready. "I dare you to flinch," she says.

H. Pompson starts rocking. His knees are drawn to his belly. "One door and only one, and yet its sides are two," he whispers. "I stand. I stand. I stand at the door and knock, knock, knock!" He covers his eyes. "Please pass by. Please pass over my door!"

I keep my finger near the bell; my father needs to be about when men behave like this. But I worry more for my father. I sense that the ocean is also calling to him. I learn again why he doesn't want me to talk with the dead souls because much of what is still inside them has yet to be rescued.

"They are not free people," my father had said.

I pull back my finger. I do not need to disturb father's rest because of the likes of this H. Pompson.

H. Pompson unlocks his knees from his arm and uncoils them from his chest. "May I?" he asks Bethanal.

Bethanal again opens her blanket and her arm to him.

"I must say that I am sorry," he says to me.

I shrug a nod but say nothing. I'm still nervous.

"And I must thank you," he snuggles to the girl. "Satan's Snakes look right dreadful in the pinch," he says.

"You're welcome," Bethanal says. "I don't get thanked for too many things I do around here." She looks at me as if I need to stroke her failing confidence.

I nod to this and for good reason. I show her respect in my expression for saving the man.

"They still fight in me. They tell me over and again that my maiden has jumped off the castle wall to her death. They giggle at how they torture her child. How they own my children. But they lie. All they do is lie. When they lie they speak their native tongue! As the Good Book says."

"What are you talking about?" Bethanal takes his arm and holds it tight.

"Vlad The Impaler returns. The 14th century Transylvanian Count lives."

"A vampire story?" Bethanal questions.

"You think little vampires are scary? Look at your heart. Vlad impaled thirty thousand in one day! He walked among the dead. Eating and drinking among them and, I might add, eating and drinking of them. He was called the Son of the Dragon; the Son of the Devil, but what he did did not come from Satan. If anything, he taught Satan. What he did, he did because he liked it! It has well been said that Satan needs the creativity and invention of evil men to carry out his plan of destruction and chaos."

"Why did the people let Vlad get away with it?"

"Some tried to defy him. It's said a group of Turks didn't take off their hats out of defiance so Vlad had their hats nailed to their heads."

"Did this inspire the Inquisition?" Jaffnel asks.

H. Pompson ponders. "Maybe it did young man. But the church endorsed the Impaler during his lifetime. He did stop the invasion of Islam, for example. Maybe the church didn't know that he just liked to kill."

"Catholics," Bethanal shrugs.

H. Pompson looks at me.

"So you think Vlad is Count Dracula," I say. "Europe's first vampire?"

Bethanal becomes disturbed.

Pompson shakes his head. "You're missing the point." The Impaler's evil inspired the Dracula story. But in this case, as in many, the reality of the human condition exceeded its evil proceeder. He was worse than creative minds can fictionate!"

"Excuse me Mr. Vampire-Believer," Bethanal releases her arm from his neck so she can see into his face. "Sucking someone's blood and killing them is pretty bad!"

"Well said. But Vlad went… how should I say? He went beyond that. He decapitated people and skinned them alive. He boiled them in tar and oil. He dismembered them. Eviscerated, burned and disfigured them and laughed while doing so."

"I can picture the burning impalements," Jaffnel says.

Bethanal looks down. She takes her warm arm from him.

"Don't like reality? Want me to stop?" H. Pompson asks her.

"I know reality." She looks at her hands.

I look at the buzzer. Not because of the story. It's sort of a gimme that it would take something pretty bad to inspire Bram Stoker's Dracula. I look to the buzzer because the eels are circling and causing swirls around Defiance. In the darkness there is organic scent of great decay. This man, this H. Pompson, he speaks of evil men and Satan with authority and it seems to ooze off the stern of Defiance as if the boat itself was in the food chain of the eels.

Satan's Snakes heed his tone. They seem to respond to his vibration, despite the fact that he has only spoken of an evil from the heart of mankind. H. speaks not of an Anti-christ, but of an entity that is in true league with Lucifer.

I take my hand from the buzzer. My father doesn't need this. I look at H. Pompson and it is in his eyes. He has seen the Satanic. Seen it befall his maiden. Seen it at the doorstep of his house.

"I'm from an old country," he says. "Upon our land has risen such old evils from the Darker Beginnings of time. It starts with the ideas. Then action figures and then pets. But it ends with impaling. What they thought was disposable, became the invitation to something they couldn't control."

"Sacrifices," Jaffnel says.

"Sacrifices," Pompson concurs. "We rose them. They are the only creatures on our planet that found our doings attractive. We invited them. Our citizens were openly drawn to them. Then they did what they do best. They punished mothers by making them eat their children. They took away all will to fight. They killed valor. They helped us seek the sweet surrender scented with immortality at any cost. Satan's siblings promised relief from what the people had become."

Bethanal looks at me and shakes her head slow, writing off the news as falsehood to me so as not to rile our imaginations. She thinks it isn't worthy of being in the logbook.

"They first made us fell the dead tourists cathedrals of what used to be France, Germany, England and Switzerland. Then the great cathedrals of Italy, where the church used to be, even though they were empty. Even though nobody worships in them anymore, even though they have been owned and maintained by the governments for a long time. Even though they are tourist's attractions. But why would the creatures frenzy G-citizens or Gitizens to turn over every stone and crush every symbol?" H. Pompson ponders his own question.

"That is why I went to the Family Book," he says. "My genealogy book, which hadn't been opened for over a hundred years. I needed to know if this was my fate. I read that Bible. I then found a secret church and then I found the Christ. The Jesus who is the Son of God. And this Jesus spoke to me after I asked to be called his own!"

This sounds better.

Finally, I relax.

17

Beyond Moloch

Timmons presses the infection out of his stump of a finger and nods in grave approval. Then lifts his eyes from us and looks back over the blackness we sailed through.

How long had he been listening? Who is on the watch? I think this as I down-class the confession of H. Pompson.

Bethanal and Jaffnel hear it too. The evil of H. Pompson's story is in their eyes. Such evil is harder to endure than carnage, fires, cannibalisms and creatures.

"Tell us of the underground church," Bethanal asks, seeking some good news.

"Tell you? Tell you what? Tell you that they all are slain? Tell you that I, their stupidest and most naive member, am their sole survivor? Tell you how my wife…"

Bethanal weeps.

"Oh Missy Boo Hoo! Are you blubbering away on my account?" H. asks. "Miss Misery! Are you pouting away my morbid mishaps? Oh, well done! Where were you when we needed to be humbled? I should have known, as a patron of the books, that sending us… sending us to the shipyards wasn't history repeating itself. We were not pilgrims! We were not going to a distant land to spread our message of love, peace and the forgiveness of sins. We were not sent away for being offensive to the king and his mice!"

"Your journey was out of convenience?" Timmons asks.

"Yes. Convenience! It wasn't from the heart. It came out of promise and not out of pain." H. Pompson says. "I for one should have known. I've read the pilgrim progress to God. It was a dismal affair. Even King David, God's Heart Man, was chased and hounded most his life. Lost his own sons. And our Puritans who came to America? A scarred, raped, mangled, slit-nosed, lopped ear, nub-fingered lot of them couldn't talk, shake hands or walk straight because of the tactics the soldiers had used to defend the King's right to divorce!

"Yet my church, just waltzes up and boards the ships unmolested and uninitiated. Oh sure, they jeered us, urinated on us from the rooftops and threw stones. But they couldn't harm us. Do you have any idea how angry evil gets because it cannot spiritually violate the property of God? But in their insolence they even had strength. They don't like to be uninvited."

"Like what?" I ask. A part of me needs to know.

When he looks at me and I reach for the button to wake my father. He too looks at the button, but then he levels his gaze. "I hail from a world where the humans of humanity are not as they should be."

This paralyzes me. I can't push the button.

"It's like that everywhere," Bethanal says.

H. Pompson stares at her. "May I make an observation?"

"Yes."

"It will cause you distress."

"I can't get hurt any worse."

"You're fat," he says.

She nods.

"Real fat," he says.

"I know!" She nods bigger, bulging the flub on her neck up under her chin.

"And you're probably not alone. Your home and your church had many fatties. Right?"

"Yes," she says, getting her voice back.

"Your country grows plumpers because being a lazy pig

and eating the pudding is still kosher in the kitchen. Church picnics. Eating socials.

"Potluck dinners," I say.

"Fellowship dinners," Bethanal corrects. "Using luck implies gambling."

"And many more," Pompson says. "Your American church is the ultimate sports restaurant, without the nectar of Guinness, of course."

"Guinness?" Bethanal asks.

"Beer," Timmons answers.

"Oh! No! Heaven forbid!" she says.

Timmons and Pompson look at each other. Then at me. H. Pompson leans to Timmons. "She means that?"

Timmons nods.

H. Pompson looks at us. "So why can't you believe that we, on the other side of the splash, could become the opposite. The good diet became a grand one. The grand exercise became the next obsession. The final generation became fixated on thin. Somewhere between Mr. Existentialism and Mrs. Nihilism, we fell in love with the culture of macho masochism. An indulgence of a much more unusual kind. All denying what the human function is. Imagine a culture where any eating translates into ugliness? You see, both our countries feed their pain."

Bethanal nods her head. Disorder is never alone.

"The gruel replaced the grog," H. Pompson says. "Areas of the female body that made a business out of being beautiful became undesirable. Wrist bones. Pelvic bones. Knees stick out on legs like buckets in the middle of a mop handle. Breasts and buns withered away. Ribs surgically removed. Starvation became the banquet. Taste for us became as rare as an uncut apple pie at your yankee-doodle church picnic!"

Bethanal looks at her blanket. "Apple pie," she sighs. Her

hands turn palm up like a plate.

"Our culture of weakness proved no match for them. Their jutting ribs and arched back of vertebrae became the ultimate object of desire, the next surgical target of all who wanted the extra twist. The final step in the long marathon of decay. The withered demoniac became the desirable."

"Then what?" Timmons spoke from the mast.

"Then the Goth of the underworld feasted on their brides. They danced them down the aisle."

I look to the east. I did it out of need. Maybe the others followed my lead, my quest for the comfort sunrise. Maybe looking the same direction made us remember why we are all on the same boat.

"Bridegrooms," Bethanal says. "Where are the men?"

"That's a good one," Pompson says. "Hard to find a man after a century of female schools; in a culture well degraded beyond the worship of the sacred feminine."

"The poor children?" she asks, just a breath below a whisper.

"My dearest. You don't see?"

"What?"

"Children you say?"

"Yes?"

"Tell me. What do you think happens to children in a world beyond Moloch?"

"How is such thinking possible?" she asks.

"Because the impossible to believe is now very believable," he looks to the darkness. He tenses and we see him struggle to control his flinching muscles. And then he turns back to us. "They believe that the raw flesh of a child does not add to the weight of an adult."

He inhales and we know he is going to tell us how this came to be.

18

Blood on the Doorpost

We look at our feet or anything we can find to avoid the eyes of the H. Pompson.

His eyes somehow cut through the darkness. But we cannot shut out his words.

We work to avoid the eyes of a person who had seen his neighbors open and welcome the Abyss of Hell. We work to prepare our ears for the voice of the missionary, yet we will him to stop talking.

But Pompson doesn't stop. He keeps describing. He keeps explaining as if we fools were still asking questions.

In the end, after his throat became too sore to speak, he turns to Bethanal, their eyes mere inches apart. "I'm so tired," he says and he rests his head on her shoulder. "Blood on the doorposts. If you open, open, open the door, they will come in!"

Pompson closes his eyes and is in deep sleep.

We dare not wake him.

He may never wake.

No one would blame him.

I nod to Timmons and Bethanal. "He is in deep sleep now," I say.

"He's beyond demise," Timmons says. "Such descents into maelstroms have no returns."

She looks at us.

I read her mind.

"I should have let him drown," she says.

I nod.

"Don't write this in the log," she says.

I nod. "I will write only some of his story in the log. But we must not tell my father or my mother the other stories. We will take the responsibility of not putting these images into printed word."

"People are only so strong," Bethanal nods.

"If we write this," Timmons says, "I worry that the log will someday find its way into the hands of history. And just as we went beyond Vlad, and beyond Moloch, so we will find a way to go beyond the now. This cannot be! Not ever!

"None need know that entire continents embrace the bone, skin and sinew and the powers of this present darkness. Powers that reduce mankind to organic tinsel for torture, tying and twisting perversion into the weakest of creatures!"

"Okay." I say. "I will only sketch it." I take up the log and open it. As I write, I am afraid that the images will sink my father deeper into his galley chores. Maybe he's known of H. Pompson's culture for a long time. If that is so, I understand his descent. I am thankful for his burden to keep it to himself.

He must never be alone with H. Pompson, whose mind seems free only when he is honest with his past.

I write only the following:

Defiance, 4th Watch. Two hours before sunrise. North by northwest. 1.5 knots. Bodies and bergs. No bodies sighted since 0400. Birds crying to the north. Expect to come into another grouping soon. Sir H. Pompson, British, awakes. Suicidal. Reports his conversion. Reports of evil creatures becoming physical and of perverted sexual relationships between tortured people and evil creatures. Reports the utter lack of hope and judgment of mankind. Claims religious icons are destroyed. Claims those under the mark of God are hated for their ability to overpower their molesters. Speaks of how the word, pilgrimage, deceived the church to do a mass exodus. Describes in much detail and great fanfare, the demonic dance as pilgrims walked public streets and boarded their ships. Speaks of ill practices. Evil creatures involved in bloodletting of their human partners. Of plunging bodies off roofs. Of a population reduced to skin and bone. Of obsession. Of perverted body image. Of streets lined with innards and corpses of the damned. Of killing and raping beyond death and the mutilation of corpses. Of possession and mass suicides from cliffs to mourn the exodus of children of Christian families— the only remaining children on the continent. Of rape and sodomy by evil creatures upon mankind. Of mankind begging for more. Of the last children leaving the continent that has stopped producing life to better indulge its selfish perversion.

I close the log.

Sir H. Pompson thunks his head against the outer wall of the cabin but utters no complaint. He goes into a soft, easy sleep.

I hold the pen. I look at the ink. I choose not to write how evil punishes those who won't give up their children. I close the book. I will never write such things. I will protect my father. I will shield my mother. I will deny future readers this truth.

Bethanal weeps.

Jaffnel's head is under his covers. His sock hands press the blanket into his ears.

Timmons is back before the mast. He can still hear.

The birds grow louder and take flight in and around our sails like black bats.

A frozen skull clunks the fiberglass hull at midships.

I slow Defiance. The thickness of the stench and not the floaters bring us to a crawl. I swing the helm hard to port and then starboard as if a rudder can wiggle our 30 tons through the pinch.

A few birds circle our vessel for a moment. We can hear the wind in their wings and then they are gone.

The Dead Sea Souls are all around us.

19

Iceman

A hard wind strikes from the west. It backwinds the headsail, jibes the mizzen boom and puts us into a fifteen degree heel. I heave to. The rudder churns water and our speed increases.

I lurch at the wheel to keep Defiance from the wind. I spill air from our small sails. I see ice and snow fly from their hiding places and fall into the darkness of the sea. Then I release the headsail sheet from the port cleat and loop the winch and crank in the stiff line on the starboard.

An iceberg passes eye level to the port. It's close enough to touch. It is old ice and has been at sea for a while because it has eroded magnificently. It has pillars and a long jutting arm.

Even in the danger I see its beauty. It is releasing enough phosphorus from the waterline lapping to bring color to its reddish glow. I see, Timmons, my pathetic night watch, come back to amidships.

He is clutching his harness and the rigging cutter stay as if collision is eminent. "I fell asleep!" he says. His voice is sad and scared.

It should be.

I glare at him. He almost... Then I remember. I am the head of the watch. I put us at risk by being pulled into a story during dangerous times. I listen.

All is still below. It is amazing and disturbing what my family sleeps through now. When I close my eyes I see my mother combing the hair of her young children with her fingers and telling them that it will be all right. She tells herself this too. She tells anyone who will listen. Every waking minute she has been saying this.

"Was it the Heaven that brought the wind to sweep us alongside this iceberg?" Jaffnel asks. "Or was it yet another Hell that rose to drive us upon it?"

Timmons shrugs from his stance along the main boom.

We stare at the danger of the beautiful chunk of ice.

I do not know the answer. I enter the account into the log, adding that the occurrence happened on the onset of H. Pompson's account of Europeans declaring war on church relics. I put the pen down and look at Jaffnel. "If I had to take a guess, I would say it was Hell. It seems the more active one of late."

Jaffnel points. "What's that?"

"Where?" I turn and squint into the darkness ahead to see if the iceberg has cousins.

Timmons is pointing too, then he motions me atop.

I lock the helm and I go up.

He points to the far end of the iceberg.

"Bones?" I ask.

Behind me I see Jaffnel stand.

"That's a first," I say quietly.

Timmons lifts his head and we both look.

Atop the elongated arm of ice on the berg, the ice arm that stretches over the water towards us, is a dark splotch. It is less than thirty meters away but we can see it clearly in the darkness.

Defiance sails closer, and if it were not for the calm, and the fact that we were passing the berg on its lee side, I would have been nervous. I am back at the helm.

We come closer to the arm of ice. As we sail by, we focus on the spot. "It may be a nest and have eggs," Timmons says.

I lift the binoculars to my eyes and focus them.

"What is it?" Timmons asks.

"An iceman." I hand Timmons the binoculars.

"Is he alive?" Timmons adjust the lenses, searching for the shape atop the arm of glowing ice.

"Probably," I say. "He's waving at us."

"I see him. He's a black man." Timmons lowers his glasses. "Then what is that?" he points off the bow.

I look ahead. I am concerned at the fear in his voice. I take hold of the mast pulpit with both hands. "Where?" I ask.

He points. "Two o'clock."

20

Agent Orange

I look to the ice. It is close. I hear a voice from the ice calling to us like one from a desert. I cup my hands to my mouth. "Give us a minute!" I beam my yell to the iceman. He sits. He's a cool customer.

I look ahead and go numb. It has been so long that I do not know what to do. Dizzying thoughts run through me. It was on the horizon but I couldn't place it. Without perspective, my equilibrium is rattled. "How far?"

"Can't tell," Timmons says. "Five miles?"

Then it rises and we know it is on a wave.

I go back in the cockpit with the goggles.

Timmons is with me.

Bethanal is holding H. Pompson, who doesn't look well with the drool slick oozing from the corner of his mouth. She wipes it again.

Jaffnel is shivering. "What?" he asks.

"Two things," I say. "See the ice?" I point off stern.

He nods.

"Don't take your eyes off it!" I turn from him to Bethanal. "You too! Keep your eyes on the ice. We'll need to go back to it."

"You sure that's the right thing to do?" Bethanal asks me. "We're down to dogfood as it is."

But I am gone to the foredeck and hold the sail aside.

The light is now twice as close. We are moving toward it.

"Not too close," Timmons says. "It's on something. So much for being five miles away."

We go the starboard gunnel and look at the light blinking from the orange suit of a man in the water.

We sail by him and walk along the gunnels as he drifts by to get a better look. We stop at the stern.

"Wake your father," Timmons says. "That there is a soldier!"

I shake my head and go to the helm. I look at Pompson.

"Don't wake him. He needs his sleep." Bethanal bumps her shoulder and jousts H. Pompson like a puppet. "Let's just keep going."

"Get him up," Timmons asks.

Bethanal shakes H. Pompson, but he is a rag doll.

"Are we going to turn back?" Timmons says.

"What?" Bethanal doesn't like change.

"Give me a minute to think," I say.

"Turn back," Jaffnel says.

I glance at the compass, wait a few moments and factor 180 from our heading. "We are going back. For two reasons."

"Your father?" Timmons asks.

The sails luff and we come about. We re-secure the sheets.

"What's up?" Pompson is awake.

"Agent Orange is up ahead floating in the water in a drysuit," Timmons says to Pompson. "And captain here is going back to snatch him."

"Don't do it," Bethanal says.

"It doesn't make any sense," I say and I look at the two men. "You two ready?"

"Us?"

I nod. "Or do you want me to wake my little sister to help?" I shame them to action, but they know I'm scared.

"It'll be less Kibbles and Bits if they're alive," Bethanal says.

"I'll share mine," Jaffnel says.

I look at him. His eyes are still toward the ice.

He obeys.

I swing the wheel and line up the course. I don't need to be accurate. The strobe is brighter than my eyes can handle. It has been a long time. "Luff the headsail off the winch." I point as I loose the mizzen sheet behind me and Defiance slows to a crawl.

Pompson takes a boat hook.

Bethanal holds his belt.

Timmons stands and Jaffnel shivers.

We hook the man in the water. Rather, he grabs the hook. He drags alongside and takes hold of the rubrail.

Pompson and Timmons pull. They lift him.

The orange-suited man soon wedges a foot to the gunnels.

Then I see gloved fingers come up and bend over the teak gunnel.

The head of the man in the drysuit is coming over the teak gunnels. And he has strength in his hands.

I look beyond the buzzer and to the east horizon. All is dark. All is black like space, and there is strength in the Agent Orange Man.

This could go wrong. We thought him to be dead.

"Kill his light," I say. "But don't break it."

Timmons and Pompson take a better hold and heave.

But the man who comes aboard isn't a victim. Not of any sorts. He is dressed in a full thermo dry suit. Military issue. Coast Guard orange. A strange flag patch is on the sleeve. A military branch patch. It is blue.

"I don't know if the dry suit helped him much," Timmons says.

The soldier's face is gut-acid-bleached gray. Despite his show of strength to get himself aboard, he now looks more dead than alive.

"Ice in his nose," Timmons says to me in a low voice. "He's been floating over a day. Maybe more. This isn't good."

I nod.

"No one floats over a day with icebergs without core temperature issues," Timmons says. "I don't care what they're wearing."

Across his body suit are some gashes but none seem to have pierced it. If he is dry, he will live.

Pompson nods to Bethanal, "We'll be pitching him overboard within the day."

"Quick!" Timmons nods. "This is easier when he's incoherent," he says as if we rescue a soldier everyday.

"Kill him?" Pompson asks.

We all look at Pompson in silence. Hands stop handling the soldier and go to warmth.

The soldier shakes his head. "Hey," he says.

This disturbs us. Maybe he isn't too far gone after all.

Timmons holds up his hand and I see his long bony fingers turn pink every six seconds to the flash of the rescue strobe.

"EPIRB or something?" I say.

"Good luck with no satellites!" Timmons says.

"Stomp it and…" I stop my voice. I wonder if my brothers would like to play with the light, but then I see the stress it would cause my mother and father. It would push them deeper into their traumas.

Timmons crushes it. "Overbaord?"

I nod and he splashes it.

The man moans.

"We're getting closer," Jaffnel points ahead.

I lunge to the wheel and veer Defiance below the iceberg for the second time.

We again sail by the man on the ice arm.

He watches us ghost by despite the dark clouds blanketing moon.

We see him.

He is sitting crosslegged on some black clothes. "Don't kill him!" the Icemen yells to us.

We sail on by.

21

Hawaiian Joe

We build enough speed and tack again, then we slow to below a knot and ghost up to the ice arm.

Atop the arm of ice sits a black man on some clothes. The area is carved with steps. He has been there a while.

Despite the calm, the ocean surges out from under the ice. Danger is close. The force of the water lunges from under the power of the ice. As we close the distance, the man leaps and hooks his legs and arms around the port spreader then slides down the stay in a controlled fall.

"He doesn't like the ice either," Bethanal says.

He crashes down atop the port deck lifelines, and I swing the rudder and Defiance veers away from the berg. As slow as torture, I see the headsail hang limp in the lee and then bend as wind finds her and pulls us and our vulnerable rudder away from the collision.

The black man limps back to the cockpit. He is covered in many layers of colored clothes and inside his pack made from an extra shirt is a block of clear ice. He holds the gift to us as if it were a rare crystal.

"Great. More ice to eat," Bethanal says.

"If we were a family of killers," I look at her, "all of you would be dead."

"But…?" she was going to say something despite the survivor's presence.

"If we had put our family's survival first, all of you would be dead," I say again.

They look at me, but they don't like what I say. They turn back and face the black man.

"What of 'im?" the black man points.

"Agent Orange here is one of them! He helped guide this genocide!" Timmons says to the blackman.

"So what if he is?" the Iceman asks.

I like the Iceman already.

The youngest among us moves so the man in many colors can sit in the cockpit away from the cutting, bitter cold wind.

I sense Timmons decrease his fidgeting. "We're rescuing a genocider," he says. "Okay. I can do this."

"We must tie him up," Bethanal says and points to the soldier. "He's stronger than us. And trained. That's why he came here. Why else but to command the killing?"

"Let's get him warm and find out," I say.

"Help him? We better ask the Captain," Pompson says.

I shake my head.

"I won't help him," Timmons says.

"Then go back to the bow," I say.

"I'm not apologizing," Timmons says.

"Do you feel you need to?" I ask.

He hesitates, then shakes his head and walks back up into the darkness after re-clipping his harness into the stage. He cradles his bad arm and takes his lookout.

"What about you?" I ask H. Pompson.

"I'll help, but I don't like it."

"Good. We're on the same boat then. I don't like it either."

Jaffnel has the soldier's feet elevated with three throw jackets and is shivering hard without his blanket.

Bethanal takes his blanket and leans to give it back to the boy. "Get warm," she says.

"What of his suit?" Pompson asks.

"If it's dry, we keep it on and conserve his warmth. If it's wet, it must come off or he will die."

They look at me.

"If he's wet, he's got to go below. That means waking my mom and taking her from the children."

"I wish the Captain was well. He'd know what to do," Bethanal says.

"He's well," I say. "But we can do this. We found him. That's the hardest part." I sheet the mizzen and heads'l, and Defiance slowly builds speed and heels a few degrees. "First things first. They may come to his last known position. If we can sail a few hours, we can increase their search zone to over a hundred square miles."

"Search?"

Pompson finishes drying the soldiers short hair and places his thick, warm hat on the man's head.

To our utter shock, the soldier sits.

He totters some, but sits nevertheless. His face is blank. "Azore High! We eat American Pie!" The soldier mutters.

I hold the wheel and watch Bethanal.

She looks at me and takes up the log, opens it and pens the words.

I nod to her and she nods back.

She is being useful.

"Are you dry?" Pompson asks him.

"Greenland's High holds down Big Moe. Solomon's Temple rains Mop and Glow." Agent Orange's eyes roll back to white as if weighted by lead like a dolls. Then he inhales and snaps back as if to stop us from giving him a tracheotomy.

I hold the helm fast, hoping speed will sail us from this danger. I stand and the wind cuts hard into my face. I don't envy Timmons on the bow watch at all. All is dark as we plow seawater.

"What else have you done! You need to talk soldier or you'll freeze," Pompson slaps the delirium face.

"Arf!" teeth snap at Pompson's hand.

That got the man going.

I look at my sea boots then at Bethanal.

She taps the pen.

We are all desperate for news.

The man grunts and looks like he might throw-up. Maybe he can see us for what we are. Or maybe the motion or the heel is getting to him. "Hawaiian Joe said so! California go! Ring ring ring the Ding-a-Ling Nations sing! Army ants in their pants!"

We look around. Where's Timmons when you need him? I see Bethanal scratching the words in the log.

Then the soldier strikes a tune. "They can dance if they want to! Big wheel keep on turning, Proud Mary found her lost, shaker of salt. Some claim the Woman's to blame! But her Chevy and her levy are gone. That was the day that we died!"

Bethanal scribes away, then she looks around. She sees Pompson drooling out of the low side of his mouth again, but now he is also shaking as if electricity is jolting him. "This is a waste of time," she says.

The soldier faces her and nods his head in total agreement.

We have a man on board who doesn't believe it himself.

He'll fit right in.

Agent Orange inhales. "Gump pushed Humpty Dump! Rocketman knows they've all blown. We can't kill the yellow stoned ant Russian!"

"This is why you don't listen to American Rock and Roll," Pompson says, wiping drool.

"Is hypothermia a truth serum?" Bethanal asks.

"It's not right for us to help this man. When he becomes healthy he will unhealthy us!" Pompson has sweat on his forehead. He wipes it away.

"Write it down," I say to Bethanal.

"I got it," she says.

I look at the Black man.

He is looking off the stern. He is holding his ice and watching his former home sink into the void.

22

Jews in the Stew

My father hands out a pot of warm water. He sees Agent Orange and quickly slams the cabin doors and locks himself back inside.

We hear the scratching of the lock against the wood.

The soldier gulps his warmed water and smiles as if it were the nectar of lava.

We pass the water to the stern, where the other man sits cross-legged and stares at our wake.

When the soldier smiles, the gesture widens the gashes on his face. The wounds open and bleed down.

Timmons is at the main boom above us. He catches my eye, not liking the speed but liking the haste. He thumbs me that all's well and returns to the bow.

Blood is now in the soldier's teeth as he tweaks a tune. "Tin soldiers and Nixon's com'n, four dead horses going up a hill. A bag of gold bought my piece of bread," the soldier nods and winks at Bethanal. "I wish you and I had been together."

She looks up after jotting the words. "He's hungry," she says.

"I can see clearly now the day is gone!" the hypothermic soldier sways against Jaffnel, who's shaking arms wrap himself deeper into his blanket. "Pigs in a blanket. Jews in the stew. Niggers in frosting and we are looking for you!"

H. Pompson nods to me.

I see his concern across the darkness of the cockpit for my eyes are back adjusted after the light strobe.

The night breezes are weakening. The dead are bobbing next to us in calm seas. The east is as dark as the west. Only the candescent, eerie lights of what looks to be an Aura Boreal are moving up and down the north horizon, making a dark purple flash within the shades of black against the sky.

We are cold. Ice is on the pages of the log book where Bethanal's tears have fallen as she scribbles away. Now I feel the chill as my fleece absorbs the moisture off my skin. I broke a sweat. I'm in danger too.

A lull in the wind makes Defiance turn upright. All becomes still except for a clanging halyard inside the mast, heads'l sheet riding a squeak in the stay guards, the mizzen sail luffing a light flutter and the groan of a snatch block.

I look east. To see a star on the horizon would be a wondrous gift. But the darkness of another abysmal night has settled around.

The Fourth Watch is a bad watch indeed.

Jaffnel holds out his hand, and his fingers bend for the log.

Bethanal gives it to him. Pages flutter as he shakes. He leans toward the helm and holds it to the red light of the binnacle and reads the words of the soldier's jabberings. "You write very nice," he says to Bethanal.

She smiles at me as if my scribe days are done.

I watch Jaffnel study the log in the red binnacle light. He does not look well. He is withered. "May I?" He takes up the pen.

I nod.

He sketches the rough shape of the continents. "This man knows how it happened," he points to his chart.

"What?"

He makes a dot between the bend of Brazil and the dent of Africa. "Azores," he says and makes more dots on the other side of South America, marked with the letters SA. "Hawaii and French Polynesia somewhere." Then he shades the land mass of Asia from Japan to Malaysia.

"Do you see it?" he asks.

"See what?" Bethanal looks at me.

Pompson stands and comes closer. He then sits next to Bethanal without asking.

"Call Timmons," I say.

"I'm here," Timmons is above us, looking down at the chart from the cabin deck. "What is it?" he asks.

"The soldier's right," Jaffnel speaks.

The soldier looks at the boy and pulls a blanket tight over his shoulders.

"Azores. Hawaii. Solomon's. Ring of Fire. This alone could crush the coastlines of the world."

"They did this?" Bethanal asks.

"They. Yes. He named them by name." Jaffnel taps the log book. "Gump. Joe and Nixon."

"God puts leaders in power. Leaders don't," Bethanal reminds us.

"This is getting wrong and wronger," Pompson says. "It's pointless to ponder the delirious."

"He's apocalyptic. It's the thread that holds it all together."

"You Yanks made too many movies," Pompson says.

"We didn't make the Woman," Jaffnel whispers to him.

"What?" H. Pompson leans to the boy.

"Anyone up for a cup of Joe?" Jaffnel asks, pointing at the log.

"Is it hot?" Bethanal asks.

"A Navy rat, Josephus Daniels or something" Timmons says. "He banned alcohol from his fleet way back when. The strongest drink allowed was coffee. To mock him, sailors started asking for a cup of Joe when the wanted a strong drink. It is done to this day. Well, maybe not this day,"

"These days don't count," Pompson says.

Despair is in the cockpit.

"A cup of hot Joe sounds strong to me," Bethanal says.

"Cup of Joe a commander? He's naming commanders and catastrophes in the same lyric. Someone commanded the catastrophes," Timmons says.

"Good one," H. Pompon says.

"Why not? You're telling me that someone didn't command Gump to push the fault lines and bring down the mountains? Move the tectonics? Make the continents swim again? Create new seas and coastlines?" Timmons is more than asking.

"We all got it in us," Jaffnel says.

Others seem to lean in towards him.

I close my eyes and think. *We stay out here above the abyss so the tsunamis don't surf us to our doom. We're in the only calm water on the planet. But why are the dead here?* "It must be awful near coastlines. Or what's left of land," I say. I am disturbed. Maybe we should have sailed on. Maybe.

"Finger of God," Timmons says.

"Finger of the Woman," Jaffnel taps my shoulder and speaks in my ear. "She's the Commander."

"Bruce Springsteen. Anti war lyrics? Or something else?" H. Pompson asks. "What? Aren't we in a world where everything means something? They've all blown. The Yellowstoned Russians? That means vodka!"

We look at him.

"What?" Pompson defends himself. "All Russians were drunks when they were around."

"Vodka would be nice," Timmons says.

"I'll politely refrain," Bethanal says.

"It isn't yellow," I say.

"It's not about people," Jaffnel says. "He says Yellowstone and Russia. Home of the two remaining Calderas on the geologic planet. Volcanologists know. They have blown or have been blown," Jaffnel says.

"Then an Ice Age will crush us all," Timmons says.

Agent Orange starts to nod at this with his whole body. Then he groans an evil laugh, smiles and points a finger at Jaffnel.

"See!" Timmons points at the soldier. "Maybe that's it. It'll crush the bone-rattling lot of us!"

"Greenland snow," Pompson says. "When it was gone the North Atlantic Oscillation shifted. That's why our snow didn't melt during the summers. Maybe it was Gump who melted Greenland's glaciers and flooded the Arctic Sea with fresh water, stopping the downwelling. Gump changed the Atlantic Drift. That's our big fat ice age problem."

"That's what took England's hope," H. Pompson says.

"And now the calderas?" Timmons looks at me.

I look to the east. Caldera and a witch's caldron sound too close. I see evil hands stirring the deep lava depths.

"It explains the sky," Timmons says.

"If they blew the calderas," H. Pompson says. "So much for the sun."

"It will kill the evil too," Jaffnel says.

23

The Caldera Brothers

I look up. The mast disappears into the dark. Even to glow a mastlight would be comforting, but we don't advertise. I have great sadness. The sky is dead.

"Are the stars really gone for good?" Bethanal asks staring upward. "I should have looked up more when I had the chance."

"It'll be a lifetime at least," Pompson says, especially if the eruptions caused it. Wait. We better use years. Lifetimes now won't be very long."

Around our circle, chins lower. He has a point.

The soldier still stares up.

The second of three waves lifts us. The wave was deep under the rollers, a good ten minutes behind its brother. It lifted the rollers too.

"Feel that?" I ask.

Two nod.

"Proud Mary and Margarita salt," Bethanal reads. "What is it with soldiers and booze?"

"Salt water reached up the Mississippi to Cincinnati in the 1811. It could do it again. Middle America isn't too high above sea level," Timmons says. "And the river marks our largest fault line."

"Marked," the soldiers says, staring up.

"If the Mississippi is stove in and the salt flats have flooded in the heartland, the hunger must be horrible."

"Try feeding the planet now, Mr. Nixon!" Pompson says.

"They never wanted to feed the planet. They wanted to be in position to feed the planet," Timmons says.

"It was too good to be true yet they called it Truth," Jaffnel says.

"Why Nixon? Nixon redeemed himself by serving the country instead of retiring. . . " Timmons carries on.

"Nixon, Gump and Joe!" I say.

"And the woman," Jaffnel whispers to me.

"What's that?" Pompson asks the boy.

"The Woman's to blame," the boys says.

"Who is she?"

The boy goes quiet and slips under his cover.

"We might want to think of the big picture," Timmons says. "Let's look at the writing on this man's wall."

"Good point. You're a scientist after all," Bethanal says.

"Only the prophet Daniel could read this writing," Jaffnel peeks out and whispers to me.

"Then let's look at the literal," Timmons says.

We nod.

"But that's no fun," Pompson says. "Let's just keep making it up. How else can we pass the night?"

Jaffnel comes out from under his blanket.

"They're looking for us. We're in the league of the intolerant. The Jews, the Blankets, the Africans and us!" Timmons says.

"Why the blacks?"

"They have long been the prophets of America. They know suffering. Their poets know hurt and they have a remnant that defies American materialism."

The skies awaken and gather a dark light high up. It flashes blackish greens and purples and reds. We are mesmerized.

"I don't think that's the Northern Lights," Timmons says.

"But it's spectacular! Simply spectacular!" H. Pompson says.

I look at Timmons.

He shakes his head. "This is something different," he says. "What?"

"Dunno. High particle storms are off our weather grids," Timmons nods. "And Agent Orange here is no help. He's still mixing his chemicals. What do we know? We aren't citizens of privilege from countries of promise."

"And you're saying he's come all the way into the middle of the ocean to look for us?" Bethanal asks. "Isn't a sea of dead enough for them?"

I see the man shake his head while all look at the big girl.

"It's for the boat. For our survival," Timmons says.

Bethanal looks at me with her big face. Neither of us know what they're talking about.

"Don't ever think their hatred is human," Jaffnel says.

The soldier looks at the boy. He had been doing this whenever Jaffnel chirped an insight. "I'm cold," Agent Orange says.

We don't see this as spectacular news. He's coherent but what's the point anymore.

The Caldera brothers have awakened.

24

Marked Up

Timmons and Pompson get the soldier out of his thick orange drysuit. They strip him down to a green, skin-tight, insulating clothing that shows the man's muscle and heft.

"Let's get him back in the suit. He's dry," Pompson says.

"If he comes to and wants to overcome us, he'll take us," Timmons says.

"He won't bite the hands that feed him," Pompson says.

"Yes he will," Timmons says.

"Have you seen one of these before?" Bethanal asks me.

I shake my head.

"Don't tell me you left before they had the grid?"

I don't. I just shrug and watch the men rest the soldier's right hand into some rag towels.

"He's just marked up," H. Pompson says to me as if I'm stupid.

I nod as I look at the metal stud in the middle of the man's hand. It wasn't unlike those in the nose, lips, tongues or eyebrow piercings that weird people did from California. Maybe a little bigger. But it was in his hand and looked natural.

"Do you know what this is?" Timmons asks.

"We haven't been aboard that long," I say, as I look at the titanium bar with little dumbbells on each side of his hand, but I didn't know.

"Just our luck. Foreheads are easier," H. Pompson says.

"Soldiers can't," Timmons says. "They get the good stuff." He brings his knees under the rags and lifts the hand. He pulls out a knife.

The soldier looks at him. "What are you doing?" he says as he holds out his left hand for the knife.

Timmons looks at me.

Pompson shakes his head and scootches back.

"We thought you were pretty far gone," I say. "But we can't have your Marker beaming out its stink."

Agent Orange wiggles his fingers. Despite the dark, we see them invite the knife.

"We're in no mood for trouble," I say.

He nods. "Neither am I. Your boat. Your rescue. Your rules. I'll do it."

I look at Jaffnel.

Bethanal lowers her eyes.

I'm glad it's dark. "I don't want my little brothers and sister to wake up," I say.

"We'll keep quiet. You're the captain!" Agent Orange says.

I shake my head. "Just the Helmsman."

"The Last Helmsman, huh? And you pull a person like me from the soup bowl?" he nods and looks at the others. As he wakens to his fate, his features morph out of his shock and his face becomes defined. Rigid. Veins in his neck grow. His hands move fluidly and effortlessly. He is under control. He is healthy.

"Give him the knife," I say to Timmons. I look to the buzzer. Too late now. We are beyond bad memories. Either way, I'm tired. Weary of the journey. I think of my parents and who they used to be. Maybe I am next to settle into the fog. Maybe we all are.

"What's your name?" Timmons asks.

The soldier looks at him as he takes the knife in his left hand. "My friends call me Rottman."

"You kill your friends?" Pompson asks.

The man lowers his chin and sees him out of the edge of his eye. "I have no friends," he says.

"You do now," Jaffnel says.

Rottman holds up the knife. "Any matches or fire?"

We hold still.

"Anything to clean the blade?"

Timmons sloshes a flask. "I use this on mine."

Rottman takes it and nods for Timmons to hold his hand under the knife. He pours it and sterilizes the blade and Timmons gets a second cleaning so nothing went to waste. Then Rottman holds up this right hand and forms his fingers into a V.

He puts the blade between the two sets of fingers. "My entire identity is in this stud. I can't get my pet a haircut without it."

"Not for long," Jaffnel says.

Rottman nods to the boy and makes the first cut through the knuckles without a flinch. Beads of sweat gush to his forehead and then his face. Then his neck and his adam's apple catch the faint albedo and shine in sweat.

Bethanal puts a hand to her face, but no one else moves. We have all seen worse.

With the blade stuck in the bone, he turns from Jaffnel to Timmons and makes another hard cut, severing the ligaments. He turns to Pompson as if to showcase his training, grunts and twists the knife and breaks apart his knuckles.

"Ouch!" Pompson says.

"If it's lose two fingers or a thumb. I'll keep the thumb any day," Agent Orange whispers and eats the pain. He nods, then turns to me. He slits the blade the last inch down to the stud and after two final zigs, he exposes the rod connecting the studs. "Lose this or lose my life! Right, Helmsman?"

I nod and feel Bethanal's eyes on me.

She feels inadequate.

Rottman hands the bloodied knife back to Timmons. The blade glows black purple. He pulls the Marker Stud free. "You have any medicine?

"Some Neosporin. We loaded it by the case," I say.

"Perfect."

"You're tougher than me," Pompson says.

"A Brit?"

Pompson nodded.

"No, I'm not," Rottman says. "I never survived blood on a doorpost."

Pompson lowers his head.

If he has the knowhow to send H. Pompson beyond Moloch, where could he send me? I ponder this.

The soldier's good hand takes Pompson by the shoulder and gives him a shake.

Pompson looks at him.

They both know something.

He retracts his arm and presses his thumb deep into the inside of his right elbow, cuts off the blood supply to the wound and stems the bleeding. The index and thumb on the cut hand pinch the stud and hand it to me.

I hold out my palm and take the CP nugget.

25

Eastern Sky

I watch the crew around me shred clothing and hand the strips to the soldier, who uses them to wrap his hand. I smile at Pompson, who drops a blood-soaked towel onto the deck by the gunnel scupper. We try not to waste anything or give too much to the eels who parallel our hull, mouths open to whatever comes out of the drains. They cruise like basking sharks.

The Marker is heavy in my hand despite the size. "It's heavy," I say.

"Nano Titanium," Agent Orange says. "Hard to make in a basement."

I test the weight by moving my hand. "Hard to believe. Something so small grants so much Citizen Privilege."

"It's because it's not true," Jaffnel says.

So much for him dying tonight.

Rottman nods to me to look to the darkness.

I nod back and take the string from Timmons and tie it to the Marker.

Timmons, in sheer caution, makes a loop in the string and lowers the bait overboard but will not let it get snatched by an eel.

"Why not feed it to them?" I ask.

"They follow us," he says.

Soon a body comes floating along the hull and Timmons drops the loop over the deadman's neck.

I look away and hear a song in my head, keep your eyes upon the eastern sky! It is a song of redemption to me. A song of hope. I know the melody but the lyrics leave me.

We just necklaced a Marker on a martyr so it wouldn't get eaten by one of Satan's Snakes.

The soldier wipes his nose again. The pain covers most of his mouth and chin in a mucousy mess. But the blood flow from his wound is slowing.

I think of the little ones sleeping through this night. They are sad thoughts. They will see things in their life that shouldn't be.

"What are we becoming?" Bethanal asks, growing white and leaning toward the gunnels for another dry heave.

Rottman is adjusting the pressure of his tourniquet.

Timmons goes to the bow.

Bethanal returns from her lean and Pompson re-adjusts himself under her arm.

Jaffnel stays under his cover.

On the stern deck sits the Iceman with his back to wind. We don't even know his name.

I finish with the log. I close it.

The soldier seems relieved.

Not wanting to appear like anything more than another iceberg if we are picked up on radar, I slow our speed to about a knot. I take hold of a back stay with my free hand and step to port to see along the gunnels toward open water ahead.

The water is still like tar. A whisper, faint with moon glow, refracts on the surface but there isn't enough albedo to see past the first wave or two.

I see no horizon and I find myself looking to the eastern sky once again.

"What's over there?" Jaffnel asks.

"Where?"

"Where you look a lot."

Bethanal snores.

I want to answer, but I do not know Rottman. I know his metal, but now Jaffnel and I are alone with him. And being alone with someone is different.

"Hope is over there," I say. I notice that Rottman has his eyes on me now. But I stay with Jaffnel.

He is more harmless and I'm tired, cold, hungry and a little nauseous from the surgery. Either way, it's two of the youngest near the strongest.

"What's hope to you?" Jaffnel asks.

I think but a moment. "It means it can come to pass when I am at the helm."

"What's it?" Rottman asks.

I look at him and I am tired and scared. "The end. And if this is the end, I mean, really, can the Kingdom of God come on such a night as this? What else but pure evil could have the hate to send a soldier like you deep into sea to kill a family like mine?" I look at Rottman trying to sound smarter than the salty, scuzz-cup in front of him.

He looks away.

I speak on. "And if it is evil that sends such a soldier, then who or what is in charge? Is it just another two-nickel killer who won a 30% vote? Is it another baby killer? An AntiChrist? Or The Antichrist?

"And has any stuff, any weird stuff, been happening at all? What I'm asking is simple, Rottman. How can I find out the truth about these times when I'm on a boat in an ocean? I see the dead, but I don't know what is unfolding. I'm too far removed from the catastrophes to render an interpretation."

I looked over at Rottman, who is now snoring next to Jaffnel.

Neither heard me.

At least I heard myself.

The breeze freshens and builds a small wave pattern opposite of the rollers coming from a distant storm and causes a pitch. The stars are hidden beyond what looks like cirrus ice clouds. Lightning from below the southern horizon strobes in them. But there is no thunder.

Time passes.

Pain wakes Rottman and he leans up. He is easiest to see because his orange drysuit. "You tired?"

"Cold only," I say.

Stench crosses our hull and we both cough mucous. It is from above and I bear off the wind some.

"Toxic. Even way out here," he says.

"It's from dead eels," I say.

"You know a lot."

"A lot of ugly. What's your story?"

"Why? Don't you think you've had enough tonight?"

"I write all the stories of the rescued in the log." I nod to where we keep it.

"It's a thin log book."

"Most who have a story are dead. But you are alive."

"Yes."

"We saved you."

"That doesn't mean you know what's going on," he says.

"What do you know?" I ask.

"What do you know?"

"I know we're not the first to see our leaders martyred, churches burned, continents go to cannibalism, cities fall into the sea, the apex of disease, the rise of Satan's Snakes, the onslaught of demons to devour the offspring of the reformation. I know I'm not the first to see the water go to grease disease because of slain saints. Am I leaving anything out? Don't tell us we don't know. Don't tell us we are safe. Don't tell me that someone can protect anyone from anything anymore!"

"So you really don't know? You really don't?" he looks at me.

I shake my head.

"Does your father?"

I lift a shoulder? I hear a rustle behind me and I turn. I see the white eyes of the man from the iceberg.

26

The Petrified

The soldier leans forward. He slurps the last cold drops from the mug before they freeze. He looks around and nods. "The boat is more pleasant than the sea."

Jaffnel is watching from a crack in the blanket.

"I don't know anything about Israel," I say. "It is at the crossroads of Africa, Asia and Europe, but still I know nothing."

"Africa is the best off," Rottman nods to the Iceman, who sits right behind me. "They were the worst off when it began. But they're agrarian; used to starvation. The earthquakes of the Sahara stunned the world. They were beyond measure. Moved the African continent 21 miles to the southwest. Pushed waves deep into the Amazon basin. Wrecked out all Mediterranean cities. Tsunamied the Mississippi beyond Indianapolis from the south. The east wave reached the Appalachian Mountains. The only survivors on the coast are the snakes. They're all fat now. Probably shedding old teeth and growing new ones every day like the Megalodon of old."

"The snakes were before the waves," Jaffnel says. "He knew."

"That's the thinking. Because of his prediction, the people made him a prophet. They made him powerful. But he wanted them all. So he granted the Ticket To Ride."

"Why?"

"Doesn't matter. Anything before Sahara doesn't matter."

"What happened in Sahara?" I ask.

Rottman looks up.

The African nods.

Timmons is here. He is sitting on the cabin top. It's hard to find a good watch.

"The Petrified rose from the depths. Like rocks being shaken in box of sand the stone trees came up. That's what happened."

"Petrified what?" I ask.

"You haven't seen the pictures?"

I shake my head.

"Thousand foot trees, branches and all petrified in stone. Not skinny trees either; they have trunks bigger than stadium bowls. Sinking sand flooded the wells and river systems where the desert water ran along the strata. Now the desert isn't a desert no more. The rivers are topside. Lots of lakes. Much is new. Green. Water forgives. But the rock trees appear heavy enough to wobble the earth's rotation. Some are a quarter mile tall!"

The man behind me nods to this.

I write it down. "What's your name? Or do you want us to call you Iceman."

"You can call me Isaac," the man says and moves to my side.

I write that down too.

"Everybody knows what it is," Rottman continues. "It has them scared. Has us scared! That's why we EMP'ed the lights. Unplugged the internet; why we corralled people into manageable groups. Cities of Light. That's why MARK UP came to be and was implemented. A soccer mom came up with the slogan. Get it? Implemented! But some photos still got out."

"Of stone trees? So?"

"Yea! So this! One of the trees. The biggest. Went green when it hit the air! How many gardens do you know that can do that?"

"What of the Africans?" I asked, missing the point.

"Dunno," Rottman nods to the man. "Do you?" he looks to Isaac.

"Sum. Da young and da old is dead. The weak, the innocent and the dumb is dead. But we can't go to our stone forest. None can. Bot we believe! We know of the tree!"

"Eden?," I say to myself.

"Looks like it. I'm not much of a Bible nut," Rottman says, but it makes the utopian trees of Pandora look creepily similar. Except you can't burn stone. Green or not!"

"You're a nut without the Bible?" Jaffnel says. "No wonder you took The Marker."

He holds up his hand. "Not any more."

"What of the Middle East?" I ask.

Rottman looks away. Then toward the hatch where my family is sleeping.

"You can tell me." I take out the log.

He shakes his head. "How long have you been at sea?"

"A long time."

"Don't longtime me, Helmsman. Give me a time frame."

"We left when the churches in our town were burning." I say and look a Jaffnel for some reason.

"Holy shit," Rottman says. "Then I'm not going to tell you. You need to enjoy what you don't know. You got out during the power outage? Unbelievable!"

I nod.

"Be content with bliss. And for the record, that was three years ago."

"I need to know," I say. "You're like fresh air!"

"Then open your book, because I'm not saying it twice."

I take out the log and open it. It has been three years of silence.

Jaffnel takes the blanket off his ears.

Timmons comes around and sits by me with Isaac to be straight on with the man.

"I have been in the system. I have access, so I know what I'm talking about. If you shut up and listen and we'll get through this."

We nod in the darkness.

He inhales. "Israel's God is alive. Alive and on the loose. These ships? All the sunk ships below us on the seabed? The crowded ones? The packed? They let them go. And we didn't make anyone bend the knee to get on board. It was a loose, loose day. But when it's damned if you do and damned if you don't, you always do. Especially where God is concerned. At least that's what we thought. We wanted them gone!"

"So the boats were going to Jerusalem. Jerusalem is Plymouth Rock?"

"It has hundreds of names. Code names. But yes. And no. We blamed everything on Jerusalem or whatever other Jewish cities they can think of. And we have our experts who show the world how every bad happening is because the Jews and Israel. But even that doesn't slow down the exodus of people, every last one of them willing and ready to die on their quest for the Holy Land. The crusades had come again. So we let them go. We let them go to the coast. Ticket to Ride! Let them board and let them walk on water! Good riddance! It's what we believed. Like anyone could survive the coast. But they did. And so did their ships."

"G-12 is using the Bible?" Jaffnel asks.

"I think it's G-18 now. Global Eighteen. But the Bible is everyone's truth book. God isn't. The Bible is. Bibles are everywhere, you know. Point being, the leaders showed the Temple burning but not being burned up. Like Moses' bush or whatever.

"But it's just a Temple. We see it every day. So the faithful go and good riddance!"

"Then why are the seas full of the dead?" I ask.

He waves me off. "Then comes the quake. India is devastated by enormous waves followed by massive starvation. Sri Lanka is a sand bar. The skyscrapers of China and Malaysia played falling dominos. Factories are down. No electricity. It's tough times. And all this when the Temple is on fire without burning up. Linking God to the destruction wasn't that difficult. It's probably true!"

"It not just America's doom?" I ask.

"No," Rottman says. "God is on a worldwide campaign!"

"So the people on the boats should have made it!" I say. "They were at sea when the world shook. They could have survived the chaos like Noah!"

"Noah's neighbors now have torpedoes," Agent Orange reports. "If we go down, they go down! No Nurch can dodge death from us."

I look around. "You mean, none but us?"

He looks at me and shakes his head.

27

Millennial War

A sense of pride and purpose, things that seemed impossible a mere hour before, surge in me. I look around in the darkness and feel strong. I feel the power of the plan of my father and his friends for the first time. I feel brave. "So that's why we did the blackout!" I point to the darkness around the boat.

"Yah, right. Like a bunch of Bible Bums can time a world-wide blackout? And maintain it? That's a good one! No, stupid. The Man gets credit for that. Him and his rats. All circuits are destroyed. All factories that make circuits are down. Finished. No nukes. No fancy weapons. No bullets. Guns galore, but they're just metal clubs because the Peace Leader and his cabinet. 'Make it hard to kill and people will live in peace,' they had said. The media sold it and people bought it. He shut down the plants that made the bullets. And I'm talking shut them down! Capped the key chemicals. There were 9,000 special ops and sequenced explosions by G-18 military elite during the three day internet blackout on munitions factories. Needless to say, they're still not up and running. What bullets people did stockpile are long gone, blasted at snakes and neighbors."

"And who did this?" I ask.

"He did. The Prince of Peace, but you can't make an omelet without breaking some eggs."

"When?"

"You mean you really don't know nothing about nothing?"

I nod my head. "That's me. Us. Not them so much," I look around. "But us," I point at the companionway door.

"I suppose it's still happening. So you didn't miss much. Except getting killed."

Jaffnel and Timmons seem to know something. "We didn't believe it," Timmons says. "It was beyond our imagination."

"You'd better believe it. Believe in Israel! Let me back up. Survivors of India march north. Well over a half of them survived. On the shoulders of the soldiers perch the skulls of the slain. They hack women and children in half. They smother man flesh in salt and sling legs around their necks. They do the same with arms, tying them at the wrist. They now have food. There is still plenty of salt. Salt is everywhere. Torsos of women and children covered the land as they crossed into Stanland and joined the Chinese.

"They fought there?"

"They joined there. Hindu, Muslim, Buddist, Communist, and everyone in between, walking shoulder to shoulder, heading east toward the Intolerants. They call themselves something else now."

"What?"

"Who cares? Continentals, I think."

"How big?"

"Big. When everybody is on one team, the one team is big. The army went horizon to horizon. The army covers all of northlands. Corner to corner. Shoulder to shoulder. Gazillians deep. Eyes all fixated on one thing because God showing up and the natural catastrophes united all."

"And this is sustained by feeding on women and children? You expect me to believe this?" I ask.

"Mainly women. And you're getting the watered down version. Welcome to the Millennia War."

"From the north, what's left of Europe's men march south out of the ice toward the Med. Once at the Mediterranean Mud Puddle, they move west towards what was Gibraltar. Now it's a land bridge. Others go east until they meet with the other continents. Nearly sink the country. Men and boys alike. They devour as they go--like locusts. They never stop. A weak soldier becomes an eaten soldier. It's a motivation strategy."

"So Israel is gone."

"No," the soldier said. "Israel made a stand."

"Against the army of the entire world?"

"The entire world!"

"Oh. Well they have guns," I said.

"Nope. Don't need guns. Just some uncanny technology."

"Nuclear?"

"Dream on. After he manufactured 1.5 PFD's, that's one and a half million Proton Flux Detectors, nothing radioactive survived the clean-up. No guns either. But Israel had stuff never seen before. Remember, there hasn't been an eye-to-eye battle since 1860's. That's the American Civil War. The carnage of killing face to face became the passion that drove the entire conflagration. Plus," he pauses, leans over and looks at H. Pompson to check his sleep breathing. "Plus, Israel still had their children. Israel has masses of children and families. So Israel had something worth fighting for... and for the Continentals? Something worth killing for..."

"How did Israel do it?"

"They lined up and faced them. You see, Israel has two generals. And these men are..."

"Stop!" I say. "I've heard enough."

"Mighty generals, I might add, and..."

"Please stop! I've heard enough." I'm begging him now. My voice cracks.

"But I didn't even tell you how they won."

Rottman didn't have to tell me. Or maybe he did.

I try to not listen. Jaffnel and I stare at each other with our hands over our ears.

Rottman keeps talking to Timmons and Isaac.

Me and Jaffnel hold our heads. We go blind with tears. We taste the acid of our deepest guts. Feel it rot our teeth. Feel our skin go cold, numb and then sweat.

But Rottman speaks on and on.

Timmons can stand it. Maybe hearing something worse makes his bad tolerable.

I stare at the eastern sky. No longer am I afraid that it will never glow in sunlight. Or never give birth to a sunrise after these horrible pre dawn hours.

I am now afraid that daylight will come.

I am afraid of the glory of God.

God is alive. He is back on earth.

I begin to prepare my heart.

28

Two-Dead Carnival

The soldier talks, giving details of human degradation. He speaks of horrible things. He checks off known items from the prophets of the Bible about these types of days. Stuff most anybody with a third grade reading level would know from a decent Sunday School teacher. I enter the following...

Rottman talks of armies, billions strong, haunted by nightmares that cause internal bleeding and snap ribs through skin. Armies afraid of going to sleep and becoming delusional and harming each other. Of getting burned and strangled in their sleep as they surround Israel.

He talks of bugs and parasites. Fleas. Ticks. Spiders. Roaches and rodents. And new kinds of biting insects, reducing the numbers of the armies. Of alkaline and acid-flood rains that were followed by temperatures so hot that the ground hardened and cemented in the legs of Continentals who had gotten stuck. They were baked in an hour. He says armies behind the baked stretch on as far as the eye reaches have all gone blind. But still they walk arms forward, following the scent of food to bring to their mouths.

He talks of Israel and weather technology defends Jerusalem, the last city on earth with no walls.

The generals of Israel have come. They caused great suffering and then how they were murdered at the Peace Summit by the Peacemaker. But they gave the Peace Man a fatal blow. Blood spews from the severed artery in his neck. Cameras show it, but the Peaceman does not die.

All realize then that he is immortal. All know that the armies are caught between two eternal forces that had begun fighting long before the time of man. Mankind is now in the War of the High Heavens happening here on earth!

So when a global miracle occurs, it is undisputed and it unites all but Israel.

I put down the pen. "What happened to the two Generals?" I ask.

"Nothing, really."

"Tell me."

"Why?"

"It's important to me. What of God's witnesses?"

"Hey, I'm just telling you what I saw go down."

"Tell me what you saw. What you saw go down."

Agent Orange pauses and lowers his head. After a while he lifts it. "Okay," he says. "Okay I will. No one buried them on strict orders from the Peace Prophet, who brought in his one hundred highest-ranking captains of the Continental Army. The ones who saw their ranks crippled by the war came in. They came in angry with hate. The ones who lost comrades because of the quakes, poisons, plagues and famine. Theirs was a hatred beyond death." Rottman pauses.

We know he's going to say it.

Rottman looks at us. "Enemy leaders did horrible things to the dead carcasses."

We wait.

Rottman looks to sea. "Remember long ago, when all of us were busy and distracted, and we found a moment to walk the dog? You walked the family dog, the one who sleeps by the fireplace and licks the cheeks of little girls at the park?

And then comes a dog walk when the pet comes across something dead in the woods or rotted by the side of the road?"

We are still.

Rottman looks at his feet. "Think back when the world was without carcasses. Think back to the time when the dog did happen to come across a carcass of rot, stomach bloat, and riddled with maggot infestation."

We don't move.

Rottman faces us. "Now tell me why a perfectly normal, housebroken pet would go and roll in the rot?"

We are quiet.

"But they do," Rottman says. "The pets always do. Why?" He looks at me.

I lift a shoulder. I don't know. For some things there are no answers. "I don't know," I say.

"Well put," the soldier says. "Yet that's what the one hundred commanders of the Continentals did to the generals. Some say they did it to remember the lost. To mourn. To embrace death. I say maybe not. I say they wanted to wear the decay like a perfume of a conqueror. They spread it around to others.

Then it was declared, a world-wide party. Two-Dead Carnival, where we all had to give gifts in double."

"When did this happen?"

"Why?"

"When?" I ask again. "I would like to know."

"It happened the day before I was sent to sea."

"What time is it?" Bethanal asked, rolling her body to upright like a weeble and stretching. "What a quiet, peaceful night."

The soldier turns to her.

"Very early," he said. "Or very late."

"Does that still hurt?" she points to his hand.

"It's not quite all-better."

"Why there?" she points to his hand.

"I'm Peace Military. We can't shoot guns. It blows off our hand if we fire a gun."

"I almost got chipped, you know," Bethanal says. "But I didn't."

Rottman nods and looks at me. He is eager to continue.

"My parents said it was the devil's doing," she says.

"Oh?"

"I still kind of see it as the perfect credit card you can never lose. Unlimited security. I don't really know why they're making it such a big deal. For children--no more kidnapping. All those criminals need it. Sex offenders and such. It helps them to stay in line and stay away from schools. And, well, you know. It works! It's not just for dogs and cats anymore. I hope my car is parked legally. My father still pays my insurance and my mom's the best chili cook in our church. Pastor Sneff says so himself."

She looks around and stops stirring the chili pot in front of her. "Am I on a boat?"

29

Primate Spore

We watch Bethanal stare at the water and the equipment on the sailboat. She is at peace. She may be cracking, but she is in a good place. Happy zones seem to be around her. She looks to Rottman. "They tried to eat me," she says.

I look east. Will it ever come? I stare on, letting my eye drift deeper into the darkness of the utter black curtain.

"Citizen nightmares," Rottman says. "But misery hates company now. They're trying to end the suffering any way they can. So Asia enacted the Millennium Spore."

"Yea, but they're insane," Timmons says.

Rottman nods in agreement.

Timmons looks at me and then at Isaac. "They changed the coding. Someone had to be crazy to change the coding. We all knew they had it. We gave it to them. The high cost of worshiping peace and worshiping the human heart is worshiping a green planet. Asia had to do something to control their population. It's not moral to let people go hungry. All agree. It's a scary thing when a population can cause mass starvation. Threatens one's existence. We just never thought the idea would go global. Of course it's bound to happen when it's illegal to make food. But the spore? Too bad they didn't have the funding to kill more discretely and humanly like our healthcare plans of the West."

I get out the log book and pull out the pen. I put it to paper and write...

Bethanal is more disturbed now. More calm. Rottman and Timmons talk of M.S. released into the atmosphere by planes. That's the spore that goes into girls through their eyes and makes women sterile. Birth control of a much more intentional nature.

I look up.

"What's the catch?" Bethanal asks. Her wide face is lighter despite the red glow of the binnacle.

We sail on in the darkness. We are still sailing very slow as if stuck in a tar pit.

"What's the insanity part?" she asks

"Close the logbook," Rottman nods to me.

I obey. I'll just add it later.

"The Millennium Spore didn't sterilize the women of Asia totally. When it was tested on primates, the bean counters found that the spore could change the offspring by denying certain genes to form in the embryo."

"Change them to what?" Bethanal whispers.

"Well, whatever they wanted to. That's the beauty or ugly part of it. And given the insanity levels of the Asian scientists, they sure made a mess of their future."

"Why Asia? Why just women?" I ask. I don't know any better. "At that atmospheric level wouldn't the spores travel wherever the wind took them?"

"It's because the dragon hates women," Jaffnel speaks. "He hates life and life producers."

Rottman nods. "Well, we all see why it's a mess. They aren't modern with modern technologies anymore. We could fight it if we were still online. At least I think we could. But now we're in the Einsteinium prophecy. We fight wars with sticks and stones. Except for the Israeli generals, who seem to leverage germ warfare at their whim."

"The spores alter a pregnant woman's offspring to what?" Bethanal asks again.

"The Millennium Spore dropped in Asia used primate genetic compounds. Children born in infected areas are more primate than human," the soldier says. "Like I said, insanity has a face. And the name of insanity is the Primate Spore."

We all watch Bethanal rise. She looks at us, then with an agility rare for her size, she lunges and then dives off Defiance! She is overboard into the frigid sea.

Stunned, they rush to the splash.

I hold course for seven seconds as trained, then do the math, swing the wheel and tack back to her.

The soldier sees her first. He takes the line and dives overboard.

The sea is alive with movement. Eels circle. They know death comes quick. They only have to wait.

To her saving grace, Bethanal floats. She tries to dive, but her thick legs only splash and kick air.

We get her aboard and she screams. She rears her head, bares teeth and bites and writhes at all the hands that hold her like a water balloon with teeth. She screams for her right to die and to kill her own.

We try to hold her, but we can't. The cockpit is awash with her withering.

Jaffnel goes to her face. "What was your first car? The one your dad insured?"

Bethanal bats him off her with a thick arm.

His head rings from the blow and he sits hard.

She goes still and we let go of her. Then she dives back to her place and sits hard. She is soaked. Steam rises off her. She blinks. "It was a Ford Festiva. After new shocks and brakes it motored me about town just fine."

Jaffnel smiles at her.

"Did I ever tell you about my Sunday school teacher, Mrs. Visser?" Bethanal asks Jaffnel. "She told us of Te-faum and of the evil witch doctor at Te-faum's village. And a bad storm that buried and killed many in mud."

I open the log.

"Good." Bethanal says to me. "Te-faum is a good story. I wish I had the flannelgraphs."

"Tell me," I lie, "and I will write it down."

I enter the Millennial Project into logbook as Bethanal tells me a Sunday School story.

I write…

Bethanal may be pregnant with the Primate Spore. Hell is rising. The face of the beast will be born of women around the world and cause them suffering, despair and madness.

I am the First Mate of Defiance. I know am writing the last will and testimony for the near-dead human race.

I want to write to God and ask him, "How long will you stand for this? For this torture of your creation?" But if I do ask such a question, I will not succumb to the urge to entertain my heart and become another weak demander. He may not protect. But he will provide. If I forget this, my heart will overpower me and I will see myself as equal with God. I WILL DEFY the demanding spirit within me. I will endure. I will die soon, but I will die well.

30

I Scribe

The cold is upon us. Bethanal defeats our efforts to dry her. She is still wet and shivers and groans hard, taking our heat as she moans from the exhaustion of chill.

We wrap Jaffnel in his blanket and he is still. He lost a tooth.

H. Pompson sleeps. He could not be awakened when we hoisted Bethanal aboard. On the starboard cockpit bench Rottman is asleep. His dry suit looks warm. Around his neck and head is a towel stained with his own blood.

We pass another iceberg off our starboard, and it glows with phosphorus too. Timmons saw it a long way off and took me around it. It is as large as a building.

We look hard and even use the glasses, but the berg is empty. In daylight we might have stopped. Ice sustains us by providing fresh water without putting wear on our filters.

I enjoy the calm of being in the lee of the ice shelf. I hear the water hissing along our hull. The storms to the south aren't large enough to pull us downwind and we hold our line. The wind is steady and the whirl of our vane in the stern is turning a trickle.

Jaffnel stirs and sits up, climbing out from under his blanket. The air is cold and crisp and the humidity is low.

"How are you doing Jaffnel?" I ask. "Have you slept much?"

"Why did Bethanal jump? Are we in danger?"

"The times are dangerous. We must overcome these times and love life." I am trying to sound brave. Braver than I am. But I can only repeat some of the professor's words.

"Will Bethanal be brave again? Will she make it?"

"I hope so."

"How did this happen? Why do they have the power and passion to kill us all?"

"All power is given by God. We must trust God's plan."

"But his plan has let them kill all of our loved ones. They killed loved ones who lifted and loved the name of Christ their entire lives."

"God can't kill his children. Only the Snake can. We must know God better than the images we see around us. His plan is for us to love each other and our enemies. We can do that, Jaffnel."

"My dad said I must never worship the Beast. Who is the beast and why would anyone worship something evil?"

"Your father's a wise man. I don't know very much about the Beast the Bible talks about."

"My father says that when the stone statues of the Beast speak, everyone will take the Mark of the Beast. Not many will deny this mark, and those that do will starve or be killed. Is that happening?"

"I don't know," I nod to the crew. "I don't think they do either."

"Yes, you do. The soldier took The Marker. He cut it out when he came aboard."

"He did."

"Will they look for him and find us? What will happen if they find us?"

"They?"

"The ones who sunk our ships and filled the seas with the dead! What are we going to do?"

"We will endure this hate and be faithful to God. Hate is but a storm. It can't sustain itself very long." These words of the teacher come back to me now, and I am thankful.

"The soldier told you the Peacemaker killed the Israeli leaders. Rottman said the Peacemaker should have died but he lived. Do you know what that means?"

"No."

"Do you know how I survived?"

"You were kept dry by the plastic bags, insulated by the hair of your people who loved you very much."

"I'm not talking about that. Do you know how I got the bodies together?"

"No."

"What's it say in the book? You write everything in the book."

"It says you stayed dry atop the bloated drowned."

"If I tell you how it happened, will you write down? Will you write down what I say about the Beast?"

"Yes."

"On the ship they knew what was happening. They saw the dead in the waters and the smoke in the air from other ship's that were sunk. But our ship had many soldiers too. And it was slowing down. The soldiers then shot someone. So many of our friends tied themselves together at the hip and formed a raft. A human ball. They died that I might live. One stayed aboard and lowered us into the water so I stayed dry. Each of them held me high to keep me dry."

At this I could say nothing, so I took out my pen and recorded it in the ship's log. Then I looked at him.

"I have more to tell you. Our entire ship was blessed. They all had a chance to die for their faith in Lord God. It was the Peacemaker who filled the death ships. But the Peacemaker is only the prophet for the Beast. A False Prophet. The Beast needs him and milks his popularity, then he takes control like a bug and the entire planet sees him. And he makes all worship him in order to survive." As Jaffnel says this he looks at me. "Write it down."

"Okay," I say and do.

He watches.

"What Sunday School did you go to?" I ask him as I finish.

"When they hooked my father, lifted him to the church steeple as he burned alive.... he caught our pastor on fire. They screwed our pastor to the steeple with a cordless drill. We watched from the cracks in the sewer drains. Then by candlelight we went deeper into the sewers and read the prophecies over and over again. All waking hours were spent reading and listening to them being read. So we endured like the Chinese. We learned to survive like the believers under Stalin. How to understand the Bible like the saints hiding inside Islam. Or during the reign of Nero. And do you know what? It ain't near over. The Peacemaker places the lives on the alter and the Beast will kill them. On my ship, when all saw the seas of dead, they were at peace. Whether they were shot or pushed overboard, they were at peace. They were singing praises to the Lamb of God for he is worthy!"

"When is the alter call?"

"Soon. The soldier said so. He said the Peacemaker was healed. Right after him will come the Beast, and they will be equal until the Beast dazzles all with supernatural power. Then all the world will unite and worship the Beast."

"What about the numbers? The 666?" I ask.

"Who cares about the numbers? Care about this! The Beast will then torture and kill all the creation of God who fall under his influence. We Christians by then will be deep in holes, or hidden on boats like this, or be dead. But it won't stop him from killing those who follow and worship him.

"He will burn down every city in a single hour. The kings of dead sex will weep. The smoke of their pleasures will be no more. The great cities by the seas have already fallen. But then total wreckage will fall upon all lands. Cities of Light are but welfare states and those who think their health will protect them will easy pickings for the Beast. They are divided and feudal and he will kill them all."

I write it in the log, using the red light of the binnacle to form the words. And I now know who I am and I know my place, despite the efforts of Bethanal to take it from me.

I am scribe.

31

Billion Man War

The soldier wakes when the companionway doors opens and he squints at the line of faint light. But he takes the warm water cups with some floating morsels and passes them to me and Jaffnel. His hair is short and shines black with grease. No ice can stick to it, but drops form at the ends and go to crystal. He nods to Jaffnel and the boy nods back, shaking a cup in his hands.

The door closes quick and all is dark.

Rottman looks at me. "I didn't know she was pregnant. Did you?"

I shake my head.

"Soldier! Soldier! Soldier!" He smacks his head three times from his foolishness.

I knew then he had seen what he had spoken about.

"She's a heft," he said. "How'd you little people get her aboard the first time?"

"Block and tackle." I nod to the main boom ahead of us. "She was dead weight."

"Well done."

"She has a bad story," I say.

"What's it like?"

I watch her sleep and turn to Jaffnel. I shake my head. I look at the soldier. "What's going to happen to America?"

"She'll be alright. Her leader is more popular than ever after bringing peace to the Middle East BMW."

"BMW?" I ask.

"Billion Man War, and he survived a neck wound from the warmongers. It cost him a chunk of his neck. Now he has an excuse for not wearing a tie."

"What are the survivors doing?"

"Ahhh! Something to keep busy. A building project."

"And you?"

"I didn't sign up to build."

"What did you sign up for? I mean, why are you here?"

"Relax. If I was dangerous, I would have killed you."

"You look old school."

"I changed. A great organizer has come. They formed 10,000 human lines to the quarries of the east and hand-passed stone for 17 days. All non-combatants of the east form food lines for the soldiers. They built a sculpture of the face of the peacemaker. It is twenty miles long and 17 miles wide. The nose is seven times the size of the pyramids and it was done by the survivors of the BMW as a tribute to the end of war forever."

"Are any cities by the sea still standing?"

"You mean like the huge seaports of New York, Los Angeles, New Orleans?"

"Yes."

"And the overseas ports of Amsterdam and Rotterdam?"

"And China?"

"Of course, China!" the soldier says, his tone frantic. "Hong Kong! Singapore! Tokyo!"

"Yes," I said. "What of them?"

"What about this organizer?" Jaffnel asks.

I wonder what Jaffnel is thinking.

The soldier turns to Jaffnel. "Some say the architect who guided the armies to build the face is stronger than the peacemaker."

The soldier stares at Jaffnel. "How long have you been away from America?" He is frightened.

"A month," he says.

"What do you know?"

"I know they are gone. I know the cities have fallen to flame and water. They were destroyed in an hour."

"What else do you know?" the soldier barely uttered the sound.

"I know that the men who indulged evil in the cities of Babylon weep and mourn. I know the few surviving merchants who grew fat off commerce wail and cry because the great sea cities of the world are gone and will never be built again."

Rottman turns to me. "So why do you need me to tell you?"

32

Heart of Darkness

Bethanal stirs in an unsettled sleep. Her eerie moans float out over the water.

"It has been said," Jaffnel looks out from under his rim of blanket, "it has well been said that it will be unbearable for those pregnant in that day."

"This day," H. Pompson is awake. "You're a bit mixy my lad. You mean this night. Right now."

Rottman tells him of the spore.

H. Pompson closes his eyes and goes back to sleep.

"Soldier! Soldier!" Rottman hits his head. "The frailty of the mind of the weak, malnourished and traumatized. And yet I stomp still. Soldier!"

The black man comes to us and sits in the cockpit. He smiles, showing us his teeth and his eyes. "If he is gone. The big woman sleeps. This young man sees and the soldier believes. Then captain, may we go into the darkness of my land. Into the heart of the darkness of Africa?" Isaac asks.

I turn and he is beside me.

He sits grey next to the black shadow of sea.

"I read the book," I say.

He leans into the red light and I see deep wrinkles in his skin as if made by a knife. He smiles. "And what book is that?"

"The Heart of Darkness," I say.

"I know no such book. But open your notebook, for where I am is beyond the dark heart of my people."

As quickly as the soft wind had come, it has left. Our momentum fades and we stop dead in the water. Our sails rattle lightly as some small waves linger. The waves are laying down as we draw close to the ice lines.

A younger brother is crying down below.

I hear the soothing words of my mother and I know she is cradling the children, rubbing her hands through their hair and telling them that the storm is almost done. Telling them that we will soon be back home and that all will be well.

I look to the east. The dark air is clear. Vapor and fog are gone and dew points are low. On the water the waves grow smaller. I see only night.

I hope this night will weaken its eerie grip on our vessel. But even the albedo is fading as the moon lowers. It can no longer push light through the thick clouds.

I hear my father snore and more gentle whispers from my mother as she calms her son.

Around me, the only movement is in the eyes of Jaffnel, the soldier and me as we weigh Isaac's words. I sense that Timmons is laying down. The sails hang as if old moss on a southern tree.

I feel that all light of sunrise is being kept away.

"I see them," Jaffnel says. He points.

We turn and see them too. As still as ice-frosted pumpkins in a patch, the dead heads dot the horizon, their hair is silver with crystals and ice holds the light from the weak moon glow.

My eyes are long since adjusted to the very dark. If someone were to strike a match, I would be blinded for hours.

We are dead still in a sea that tells us of dreaded fates.

"Some are moving," the boy says.

"Sure enough," Rottman says.

We watch a few spin in the stillness as if they are trying to swim or fly out of the ice. Others pop down and up again like bobbers at the end of cane poles in a trout pond.

"It's just the eels," Timmons says from the cabin top. He seems only inches away. His voice carries calm and clear. Then we hear his footsteps as he comes into the cockpit.

The rigging is still. Even the halyards stop tapping the aluminum mast with their echoes.

I hear my father sleep deep. My mother is again quiet with her young children, and Bethanal had succumbed to her stupor.

I had never heard a voice like Isaac's. Yet now, in the stillness, we feel his burden.

He can carry it alone no longer.

We rally and look at him, and we see the white around his black eyes expand. His eyes protrude as if intense pressure is inside his head.

I ease to the other side of the wheel, closer to the soldier. If he could rescue Bethanal from her suicide, he might be strong enough to defend me from the darkness of this man.

"Take out your log," Rottman says.

So much for safety.

Isaac looks around. The tails of the eels are seen clearly as they break surface or snake along just below it. Many of the dead are still, for the eels are fat and sated. Sleeping in the calm, their soft dorsal fins ride above the surface like a line of grass in a sidewalk crack. Isaac is unshaken by this new world of his, which makes us wonder about the world he left.

33

The Terror

Isaac leans to me. "You saved my life," he says. I look at the blank red page of the logbook. I am not eager to enter another heading.

"And my name is Isaac with two a's."

I look at the teak grate below my feet. No wonder he stepped on a ship for Plymouth Rock. He sounded as if he were from the Islands. I was in Haiti once on a mission trip after an earthquake. We repaired an orphanage. The missionary had stories of voodoo that could curdle lemonade. Everyone wants off that island!

"Where are you from?" I ask. "How did you get here?"

"I came up because the Englishman sleeps too deep, mon. If you sleep too deep you cannot awake until time to run away is over. I am from Africa," Isaac says.

So much for my island theory.

"What is Africa like?" My question slips out.

Rottman looks away.

A silence comes. It stays so long that I am jolted back from my eastward gaze when Isaac speaks.

"Africa is empty. For too long the nations have danced in darkness and superstition, afraid of the night. For too long, as far back as our ancestors reach into time, we have bondaged women to work and toil. For too long we took their daughters as prizes and trophies into the bush for our pleasure. All men know we have done this, because they have all awakened."

I nod, remembering the Great Awakening from one of my history books.

"The Terrors have come from the graves to walk the forest. They roam at night, first only to let the Terror settle over the land far ahead of them."

I am nervous now. This isn't a spiritual awakening.

"Then they walk in the plains at night," Isaac says. "The Terror infects the minds of the living. Only den did dey walk in the daylight. Den dey become The Terror as they do the terrible!"

"What are you talking about?" I ask.

"You don't have to tell this," the soldier says, nodding at Jaffnel.

Isaac nods to the soldier but shares no passion for the events. "The risen dead have become eaters of life. From along the ocean they have come. Side by side they walked from the ocean toward the men. Calling to them to come and lay with them. Calling for their organs. Calling for their thunder. From the north to the south dey come; from the oceans and all the men go east. All go inland. We run from The Terror Walkers. For weeks we run from dem, but still they walk us down. In the deep jungles, in the heart of Africa, when we could run no more they circle us.

"All the men pool together. Da men fight dem. Their machetes are sharp and they dismember, disembowel and behead da Terror. But still they come and their touch comes and holds down the men. No men surrender. But many, many, many art caught. They catch their fear. They catch their pain."

I look at Timmons. I don't know how to write this.

"For weeks dey feast upon the men. They walk-attack with plague and disease and insects seeping from their crotches. Their teeth are sharp as if filed as they chew and tear off the genitals and feast on the scrotums of da men."

I see Jaffnel under his blanket. I watch Pompson and Bethanal asleep.

"But some of us are strong and we run. We run fast and long. But still they walk. They look at us as their prey to appease their endless appetite. In their wake they leave most men alive, bleeding out their manhood and screaming like all the women and children they have ever raped. The forest floors are slippery with blood before the maggots are hatched."

"They hold out their arms as they come. Long fingernails reach out. The wiry hair of the grave swims around their faces and necks. The sunken leather of hardened time covers their bones, hands and bodies. Hair hangs down over their gaping eyes like ocean weeds. They show their jutting teeth for their mouths are always open. Their mouths, like the barren old or man-destroyed young wombs, are open for the feeding of their endless appetites."

We are drawn to Isaac's face. Blood seeps from his eyes as he talks. His ears bleed too, as if the screams of the devoured were daggers. He uses hand gestures to show how the dead women of the graves keep their prey alive as they share in the feasting, and how the bodies of the mauled men lay withering for days as the lines of the living dead walk deeper into the interior of the dark continent, seeking the last of the living.

The dying were left to be eaten by the animals and other dead eaters that followed with more appetite.

"When a man, too weak from his machete swinging, falls down, they gather around him. The undead women hold the man down and begin the raping. They use the rot and bugs from their sex to drown and suffocate the man as they dissolve their lover victims."

I close the logbook. I'm not writing this down. They can't make me.

Isaac looks at my book. "Evraday part of da male bodies dat ever touch a woman become the coveted morsels of the appetites of the undead. Da toothless old and fanged young slowly gnaw the meat off the fingers of the men.

Nine Daughters

We look out at the open sea. Anything is better than seeing Isaac's bleeding eyes. The familiar twists and turns of the iced and eaten faces in the eely sea bring us relief.

But as we look over the water, the screams of the feasting dead and their trapped prey enter our minds and echo in our ears. We hear them beg for death. We see the lustful and dominating eyes of cruel men get licked away by dry, carrot-like tongues of undead women.

We see eyes become mere holes in screaming heads.

Isaac uses his fingers to hold back his lips as he opens his mouth and shows us his few remaining teeth.

We look back at him.

"Blood running off their eyeteeth and chins and down their necks, the Terror lifts the bones of the feasted fingers from gnawed off hands. They shake these hands and rattle the finger bones of the men like haunt chimes in the wind.

"The lips of men, smothered full of the rotted become dens for bugs passed on from the corpses. The trapped dissolve away in torture as the undead terror force sex into the mouths of their slaves and as the oppressed 'omen become the dead oppressors, they spray the throats of men with the rot and carrion from their violated, destroyed and vengeful wombs."

Time passes but all stays dark.

"How did you survive?" Rottman asks.

We know Rottman doesn't doubt. We know Isaac has more detail. Much more. We don't deny truth from a story-teller bleeding from his eyes and ears.

But if the undead did invade like a swarm, it makes sense that they would kill all.

Isaac pulls a long knife from his belt. It is a dirty, dark blade with a thick metal handle.

"Ten years ago a woman came to my church. She had nine daughters. Four died from rape AIDS before they were twelve. Four others were infected and suffering under the tyranny of evil men. Some of the men who did 'dis to them were of our church. But her youngest? The infant? Her tiny baby daughter was taken by the village chief. This chief had HIV and like many, he believed HIV could be cured by having sex with an infant. He killed the baby girl as he did his horrible to her."

I look at my feet and weep. I feel Jaffnel's arm on my shoulder. I shrug it off and look at Isaac.

"So the momma came to me for I am pastor," Isaac says. "She asks, 'Where is God when my girls die? Where is God when they cry and bleed away the nights? Where is God when they beg the men to get off their little bodies so dey may be women of promise? Even the whores of the Bible had nothing like this!' She says dis to me.

"She not the first momma to come to me in shame. But when she tells me dis, my ears were opened by God. I feel da pain of da cross like she does in her heart."

He points the knife at us. "So I gather all the men of our church and I make dem sit. I make her sit and I tell the dark tales of her nine daughters. God helps da men to hear.

"I look at the men of my church. I say, 'God is angry, and we are all guilty of taking daughters to the bush. You all know of dis woman's daughters,' I says to them and I take out dis knife as I speak and I put dis knife into the fire I have prepared."

Isaac holds the dark knife up to us.

In the red light of the compass binnacle, we see the blade turning. It is red black.

Isaac lets us look at the knife for a long time. "I then say this woman. I say dis to her when she stands before all the men of our church and village. I say, 'God is angry with us men. And His hand of power and wrath is ready to give His curse on our land!'

"I tell dese men, 'I don't want the damnation of the hand of God upon my church, but He is God and He must act soon! He will not spend eternity apologizing to da woman of Africa!' I pull dis knife and show da men of da church. Dey see it glow red hot from the fire, and I stand before the woman at the wooden block. I move away my clothing and I place myself on the block. All of myself on the wooden block. I still see the woman watching me as I cut myself clean and do my castration with the same swipe of da red hot blade!"

We look at Isaac's black-bladed knife. He shows us the full swoop of the blade.

He looks back at me. "When my time of screaming is done, I stand before the men of my church and make the woman stand again. I give her my knife and lift her hand with the blade, still hot from the fire and stained by my blood. I put it to my neck." Isaac now pulls down his thick shirt and aligns the blade with a long white scar.

"I say to the woman, I say, 'I am Isaac. I am Christian and Pastor of dis village. Do to your servant what you please, but do not no more curse da God of Heaven for the sin of man against your daughters.'"

Isaac lifts his knife and points it at us. He smiles. "She lowered my knife and became Christian." Isaac smiles big and wide, his few yellow teeth catching some soft red light.

The soldier starts coughing and lifts an empty mug to his mouth, looking for the last drop.

"You don't believe?" Isaac stands and drops his pants to the cougher. By the look on Rottman's face, I could tell he saw the nothing. He saw castration.

Isaac brings up his pants and sits. He holds up two fingers. "Two. Only two of the men in my church followed me to honor the woman of nine daughters dat day. Two."

I could understand why the numbers were low. I look at Jaffnel.

He has the covers over his head and I hope he is asleep.

"But the years did pass and as the fleeing men come our way ahead of the walking dead, my knife again goes into the fire! As our village was trampled by the man hordes escaping the witches, my church again became house of cleansing. Many men from our village filled our church. I made another fire and the knife again grew hot. I cut away all the men in my church the day before The Terror came. From the boys of age to the very old. Their woman came with wrappings and medicines and we all stayed in the church as the undead invaders passed by in swarm. We stayed on holy ground, covered in the blood of the converts. We hear The Terror walk by, dragging their long fingernails on the outer walls of the House of da Lord as they passed. Our faith in da judgment of God led us to clean the church floor with our own blood of repentance.

"But just ahead of the line of dead, the weak and very tired men fall in our streets, and we watch them get eaten by The Terror who now judge the oppression! We made all men and young boys watch from our windows so we would never forget. The Terror passed around us like water by a stepping stone in a river."

"What did you do with all the... all the stuff?" Jaffnel pokes his head out from under his blanket.

He picked the wrong night not to die, I think.

"We throw them out da windows of our church and we hope, as our doors shake when dey are clawed at, we hope dat de doors stay closed. We hear the undead grind the parts away in their teeth. We hear them sniff at the doors and windows of our church as if to smell the fear of the unrepented," Isaac says. "But we have no unrepentant souls. We have only sorrow and much pain."

Isaac stops talking and all is still. Small ripples come from the sea and quickly go their way.

I look at the blank page before me. I take up the pen. I write,

0500ish. Dead Seas. Becalmed. Dark. Isaac speaks. The Terror of undead women rise from their tombs. Zombie woman eat the African men. Only those who cut away their sin seemed to have been saved from this plague.

I put the pen down and look at Rottman and Timmons. Both are looking at Isaac's knife.

I look at Jaffnel.

"None of the escaping men came to your church for help?" Jaffnel asks.

"The Terror had them. Many wanted in, but the altar of sacrifice was at the threshold and none wanted to pay the cost of being a disciple on their day of judgment. Mine was not the only church that did this. The sinners could have been saved." As Isaac says this, he slides his knife back inside his belt.

Weight of Heavy Peril

I close the log. I am glad that my job is only to record the happenings. I do not have to make people believe them.

Isaac feels his cheek. His fingertips trace the cold blood trails coming down from his eyes. He scrapes them away like strips of dried paint.

I look over the rail and see eels at the surface. They are sleeping and still in the clear, cold waters. A large one snakes by, leaving swirls and funnels on the water. The biggest I've seen yet. If they get much bigger, Defiance will become small.

Maybe it is time to leave the dead souls. I wonder if I should tell my father, who has been a good captain. Maybe I'll make the decision myself.

The weight of heavy peril is in all of our eyes. Despite our belief in grace, despite seeing and hearing how it works, none of us feel we will survive this night.

The Summoning

Timmons rushes back from the bow. "Something's wrong ahead! Above us and ahead of us, something's way wrong!" Timmons yells. He's breathing hard. He will disturb my family.

The soldier stands and walks on light feet to amidships and looks out over the sea. Never once does his good hand let go of the rigging. He rubs snow from an extra life vest and straps it over his drysuit. He tightens it around him.

I look east, harder than ever, growing desperate to see the dawn. But the noise is now above me and it draws up my sight.

Next I feel all the crew are looking up, but none of us know what it up there.

"What is it?" Bethanal asks. It awakens her.

"Don't know," H. Pompson replies.

Maybe I pushed the buzzer to alert my family below. Maybe I didn't. Maybe someone else did.

Noise stirs below the decks.

My family is moving.

"It's up there, whatever it is!" Timmons says. "It's very high up there. Or is it close?"

The companionway doors open and the slide moves forward.

My father comes topsides carrying my little sister. This is not good, for neither are wearing a life vest. Both are tired; very tired. And they are not in warm clothes. Their hair is messed.

Then my brother climbs the companionway ladder and holds the legs of my father.

They do not notice strangers on the topsides. They are looking up.

My mother comes topsides with the youngest. He reaches his hand to me, but pulls it back as the cold touches him. Despite being held tight by the arms of my mother, he cranes his small neck and looks up.

I see his hair, plastered against his scalp by countless combings from my mother's fingers.

She too sees beyond the strangers and looks to the sky.

Jaffnel is on his feet.

A rogue wave would knock most of us overboard.

Behind me, Isaac mutters words in a language I do not understand.

The air is alive but there is no wind.

"Birds!" Jaffnel shouts. "Billions of birds!"

I look around at the dark sea for danger. Then I finally look into the sky.

It is true. The black clouds are a few shades lighter.

"It's not a fog or a frontal lift?" I ask.

"Those aren't clouds," my father says. He has his arms around his two middle children and is on one knee.

I miss that.

To the north the sky becomes more alive still with the roar of wings on the air. Downblasts swirl around us as if rotors were above. Wind displaces all stillness and the quiet movements of Defiance. And then the thunder of the cries of the fowl fall upon us.

My sister reaches out a hand to catch a floating feather.

Jaffnel points to the direction the sky is moving. "It has started."

"What is it?" I ask.

"The Great Feast," Jaffnel says.

"Lord, God!" Isaac puts his hands to his mouth. Timmons stands and looks at the night sky utterly filled with south-bound birds. He lets go his hold and lifts both hands in awe.

The birds are passing, flying wing to wing and thousands deep. They cover the expanse of sky. The roar of sound fills the sails but the boat is still.

"Do you know what it is?" I ask my father.

"Yes, I think so," he says, not taking his eyes off the immense, dominant sky.

"Where are they going?" my mother is at his side.

I look at them. It is good to see them together. Even in such a time as this, it is good. I have not seen them together in a long time. I look to the horizons for danger. I look back to my father.

My father speaks without looking down. "They are going to Armageddon. They have been summoned by the angel of God to gorge themselves on the flesh of men. The rider on the white horse has come. The dry bones will rise. The armies of man will fall. The winepress will squeeze out the fury and the grapes of wrath of God. The end is here."

"Oh Lord, my God!" Isaac shouts. His arms are raised in awesome wonder and he proclaims.

My father looks at him but a moment, then turns back to the heavens. His voice is in my ears. It sounds like the professors. It is without fear.

For a long time we crane our necks at the birds crossing the horizons.

Then the deafening cries of the birds engulf us and all thought is lost in sound and fury. The raptors and carrion-eaters scream out as if the unheralded saints and unknown poets of the centuries have finally been given voice.

And roar in cacophony they do!

We stare at each other through air afloat with down and feathers, our ears cupped as we yell our thoughts of wonder to the one's near us.

Our boat and the black waters become covered in white, snowy feathery down.

For a moment all blackness is gone.

37

Utter East

One by one we take our hands off our ears and settle back to enjoy the surge of life on the planet. It has been snakes and sea serpents far too long. Too bad the birds can't eat those worms.

As we did before the trouble, my father and I are staring together to the east, waiting for the black of night to turn. We tighten our collars as the cold settles down around us from the downblast of wind. Our ears have become accustomed to the drone of wings and the war cries of the enraged flocks high above.

I feel movement in the cockpit behind me and hear a blanket fall to the floor.

Since Jaffnel had never been without this blanket since his arrival days before, it strikes me as odd that he sheds his outer layer.

So when he walks up and stands in front of the mast, my father and I follow close behind.

A child leads us.

My father is intrigued.

Jaffnel looks east on the cabin top, the highest safe area on the vessel. "East?" he asks me as he points.

Being the expert on that direction, I confirm it with a nod.

"Then why is it light in the north?" he asks. The chaos of the birds kept our eyes from that direction.

He is right.

The high ice clouds go bright red and orange in the upper levels of the northern atmosphere. They catch light from beyond the horizon. The light grows brighter and soon the black ocean around us turns to shades of rose and yellow and then a wondrous dark orange as moving light falls on us and keeps going.

The dead sea souls glow with light but I stare not at the horror. I crane my neck up.

We see it. We can't miss it.

It is now beneath the dirt coverings of filthy ice clouds. It is white like a sun! The water is blue!

All are amidships, before the mast to get a view and in the color we look worse than otherwise.

The light stings us and we hold up our hands to shield our eyes. It hurts our eyes bad, very bad. But we cannot look away. It has been too long since we have seen color.

"It's beautiful," Bethanal says. "God has given us a new sun! But it's moving away so fast!"

Clouds billow ahead of the light and fan out like fast-building thunderheads. It is light from east to west. The sky is on fire!

I take my father's hand and he squeezes hard. His wife is near, holding a child. He draws her in with the other arm. I feel a little brother climb on me and I help him up. I haven't held him for a long time. And I haven't been held since I don't know when.

"It's been a great sail," my father says. He is brave.

It is over.

It was kill us.

Jaffnel is by us. Timmons and Isaac too. Rottman is on the far bow. The deck has color. It is gray from snow ash and needs a washing. The boat lurches a little and I know Bethanal is standing in the stern with H. Pompson.

Talk will now be short. Very short.

It is coming fast.

Jaffnel is at the gunnels. He is closest to the moments of the end of the age. He turns to look at us. His hair is a sandy blond and we see unhealed pain in his face from the fires he witnessed. He inhales. "It is the millstone from the angel of God. It will destroy the remaining cities of man."

It came at us then.

It now came under the dust atmosphere, bursting into flames from air friction. It is angling toward the top of the world with a force beyond scope or measure.

 I calmly reach for the stays to balance the eminent impact of cataclysm shock, but I can't touch them.

Below us is the water and we strangely feel that earth will soon be knocked back on its true axis by the energy of mass times a constant power.

We strangely just know this to be true.

We see our sailboat far below us in the maelstrom of rushing sea and vapor blast.

Then I, the last helmsman and scribe look around. I see us all looking to the east and light is on our faces. I look down at the the sailboat far below.

I look to the east with the others.

We see all.

We know all.

And all is good.

We are.

The End